JASON JOHNSON was born in Enn[...] Belfast, England and the USA. [...] salesman, a car washer, a supermar[...]employee, a waiter, a courier, a chair-ride operator, an apprentice stonemason, and a painter and decorator. As a freelance journalist, he worked for the *Irish News* and *Belfast Telegraph* before taking the News Editor position at the *Irish Sunday People*, which he left in 2004. His first novel, *Woundlicker*, was published by Blackstaff Press in 2005.

PRAISE FOR WOUNDLICKER

'dark and gritty'
Sunday Times

'hard-hitting'
Sunday Life

'searingly truthful, uniquely uncompromising'
Irish Book Review

'a pacy page-turner'
Belfast Telegraph

'poetry and prose from a top-class writer'
Sunday People

'full of strong imagery and language ...
a gritty thriller'
Books Ireland

'strangely moral ... short and brutal ...
an unflinching confirmation that we are our
own worst enemy'
Ireland on Sunday

'A counterblast to sectarianism and peace process
humbug ... Johnson's debut novel is a wrathful and
indulgent, slick and witty "fuck you".'
Fortnight

ALINA

JASON JOHNSON

BLACKSTAFF
PRESS

BELFAST

To the freaks, spides*, brawlers, perverts, saints, sinners and
extraordinary Romanians who unknowingly inspired this story ...
To Gerry for the use of the cottage ... To my parents for the house,
grog and dog while I wrote and they trekked a rain forest ...
To my sister Rachael for her enthusiasm for the first draft ...
To Joe for the African chant ... To my almost-wife Sinead for being
there from start to finish to beyond ... And to all linked with
Blackstaff – especially Janice, Abbey, Wendy and Rachel –
for making my day, many days in a row ... Thank you.

*Chavs, but from Belfast

This is a work of fiction. All characters are the product of the author's
imagination and any resemblance to actual persons is purely
coincidental. Some locations are real, some are not.

First published in 2006 by
Blackstaff Press
4c Heron Wharf, Sydenham Business Park
Belfast BT3 9LE
with the assistance of
The Arts Council of Northern Ireland

ARTS COUNCIL
of Northern Ireland

© Jason Johnson, 2006
All rights reserved

Jason Johnson has asserted his right under
the Copyright, Designs and Patents Act 1988
to be identified as the author of this work.

Typeset by Carole Lynch, County Sligo, Ireland
Printed in England by Cox and Wyman

A CIP catalogue record for this book is available
from the British Library

ISBN 0–85640–794–1

www.blackstaffpress.com

For Matt,
brother and old friend

Arise, those who are branded ...

Nicolae and Elena Ceausescu in song at
Targoviste Military Base, Romania,
25 December 1989. They were dead
before the dots.

1

Alina took the tube of lipstick and began drawing on her stomach. She knew it might look ridiculous, but it was worth a try. Besides, it would rub off easily. As she drew a careful corner, smiling brightly like everything was just fine, she remembered The Policy. It made her hand stop.

The Policy: The way Alina was going to make life better. The Policy was seven months old. Alina was eighteen years old. The Policy consisted of one simple rule: Do not spend money unless absolutely necessary. Alina would not breach The Policy. If she did, she'd have to visit her father.

Alina's poverty had arrived fast and complete. Her response had been to make a rule, and to tie her future to the rule in the hope that eventually things would work out. Life would require less funding and that, she believed, was a path towards economic freedom. And yes, there was some sort of textbook, theoretical merit to the idea, but nothing realistic about it. She was stretching things, but where to? She would never be able to pay off the debts which had taken ownership of every part of her body and every moment of her life. The Policy, in reality, was one long-term strategy of making things worse in the hope they'd get better. And the threats, the cards and letters, just kept on coming. They looked now like lines and lines on top of each other, a paper brick with her name on it, balanced on a small, obsolete television.

She had thought, a moment ago, how she would soon reach the dead head of the lipstick tube, and remembered that she must use as little of everything as possible. She reduced the pressure and began moving her hand again. The cosmetic application thinned and she therefore continued, she liked to believe, to spend only what was absolutely necessary.

Alina's God was sending twenty-four hours every day, but it wasn't enough. She was awake from each sunrise to each midnight, and she wished she could be awake for longer. The rest of the time, in the six or five unworked daily hours, she would hit deep sleep fast, right there in the same place where she sat, lied, searched, smiled, kissed, thrilled, drew lipstick and violated herself with a pre-owned sex toy. Alina's sleep fed on time she couldn't afford to spare, and she resented it.

Naturally, she was exhausted. Her limbs sometimes ached from the deprivation of her tiny diet, her life-sapping living arrangements and the sheer lack of rest. Her muscles, though pretty, had grown weak. The blood running through them was delivering almost nothing. She was hungry, lonely and had thus far failed, but here's an important thing about Alina: she was not losing her professional touch. On the contrary – she was getting better every day.

There's tragedy in this story of Alina. There's fear too, a constant concern that this young woman may be slain by a pervert more twisted than the truth. And yet there's another part, the part that has everything to do with that professional touch of hers. Because Alina can look at you and warm you, wrap you up in little words and easy deeds and spoil you, make you chuckle. She can move, and move you miles away from your troubles. If you could see that dark little square she lives in – that little public window onto her private life – you'd know precisely what Alina's professional touch means. It's been known to make people shake.

You'd look straight into The Policy's darkness and find Alina's full, milk-chocolate eyes. She'd come forward, looking into you, forcing onto you, making you feel like she's fast coming into your life and that she's drama, that she's as weak and as wild as the wind. She'd stretch a limb, lick a lip. She'd move further forward and bring your eyes down with her own, tipping her head and yours forward, down onto a delicate chest, onto the heavy promise of pornography. And by the time she'd have lifted your eyes back to hers, she'd be beckoning you in with her thin, graceful fingers and you'd know something about Alina's professional touch all right. People often think of that professional touch for a long time after they see Alina, and often when they want to do something hard to someone.

Outside, earlier that day, Alina had found some cigarettes on a street named after Christmas Day. She'd passed them while on the monthly walk to visit her Protector. She'd noticed the packet, that its lid was flipped open, that around half of them were still in it. She wasn't sure if she'd seen the brand before, but then she didn't smoke much. She took a left hand out of a warm pocket, bent down and picked up the packet.

People in a café across the street watched her every move, telling themselves they instantly knew things about this raven-haired stranger who found her vices on the street. They drew on coffee and crosswords as Alina tucked the box into that warm pocket and went on her way. A woman of twenty-two said something to her boyfriend – he was struggling with a verb at the time – about some people just not feeling embarrassment. He smiled and agreed, without looking up. He would have liked Alina.

The Policy didn't require goods to be found or stolen, but its single rule was honoured by Alina's stoop. Attractive girls who sucked on lollies and fingers and bottles were popular in her world, but those who sucked on cigarettes seemed to have a community of rich men all to themselves. Alina thought their special appeal might be something to do with cigarettes being unhealthy and taboo among the young in some countries. They were, she figured, a sign that a girl had taken a wrong turn, and could therefore be talked into taking more. She knew there was a place where men enjoyed girls who got damaged and hurt, turned from fit to shit. Smoking – as long as she did it the right way – was a little signal to those men that Alina might just be available for that one-way journey. In reality, she was already on it.

She finished putting on the lipstick and checked the result in the mirror. It wasn't too bad at all. She straightened her bra – it had ridden up a little on one side – and ran her hands through her hair. Some strands had escaped a soft, shining ponytail, but they were soon back in place. She put one of the found cigarettes into her lips, lit its end and turned her gaze straight ahead. As smoke rose and kissed her forehead, eight men turned their attention to the lovely pearl-skinned girl who now begged for them to come and get her.

Mmmmmm, said one man who listed his hobbies as painting, laughing and shooting. *You look so hot baby.*

Another, who had a lock of his neighbour's daughter's hair in his hand, said: *Heart beats soooooooo hard for you baby!*

Alina drew their eyes to hers, and took them all down to rest on the unruly new lipstick markings across her drum-tight stomach. Each onlooker made a quick calculation as she exhaled a thin tumble of smoke down onto her midriff. It read, in red, *$1.99.*

2

Two lads on a flat roof shout at Henry Sender. He looks up, not thinking. Shit. They might drop something on him. He smiles nervously. He hasn't a clue what they said.

'Give us the Pisser,' squeaks one, a fifteen-year-old whose teeth are dying. The other, a fifteen-year-old with no hair, points to a hedge. There's a huge red and yellow water gun. It looks like it could be used to fight in outer space. 'Throw it up, mate.'

Henry goes to the gun. It's heavy and stinks of petrol. Christ – it's loaded with petrol. 'Throw it up to fuck.' The bald one is anxious, looking behind him.

Henry knows they're up to badness, but he's not about to walk away. What would be the point? They'd soon shimmy down and get it, or him, anyway.

'Hang on,' he says, dropping his shoulder bag on the ground. It's Belfast, Northern Ireland, 7.17 p.m.

'Chuck it up.'

Henry has to throw it two floors into the air. He knows he could fail, that it could fall and smash and pour pints of petrol onto the street. One of the boys could tumble off and die as he reaches to catch it. The police could be watching everything. Too many thoughts. Forget them all, Henry. Throw it. He throws it with both hands. The one without many teeth catches it. He's safe.

'You got it?' Henry shouts.

'Where the fuck are you from?' roars the bald one.

Henry hates the question. 'Here and there,' he calls, blushing and turning to pick up the duffle bag.

'Suck on this, ye bitch,' shouts Baldie. A hard point of petrol pokes Henry on the back as he stands straight.

'Damn.' He said it quietly. He turns to face them. Another jet is about to come his way. He runs instinctively, inflammable, deciding he mucked that one up in two ways.

A little later, in a lecture hall, a woman with her right arm in a sling writes on a whiteboard with her left. The small, impotent capital letters droop towards the end of the sentence. Twenty adults watch her in silence, all considering that she's probably right-handed.

'I'm right-handed,' she says, turning and capping the pen with more skill than you'd expect. 'All I can say is don't fall down a pothole.'

The class laughs with gusto. Henry looks around and smiles too late. Yohan, to his left, can smell petrol. He sniffs out loud. It's hard to know how potent the stench is to others after you've grown used to it.

'You're stinkin, Henry,' says Yohan, quietly.

'I know. Don't ask.'

'Don't ask what?'

'Don't ask that.'

'What?'

Henry closes his eyes. He can't cope with this guy sometimes, with his big nose all over him every time they meet.

The man to Henry's right, a customs officer who rarely speaks, says: 'There's a serious smell of petrol from you, mate.'

'Yes, I know,' says Henry, and smiles. He doesn't want to sound sharp. 'I spilled some.'

The man nods. 'I hope you don't smoke.'

'Yes,' says Henry, forcing a laugh which he hopes doesn't sound as fake as it is. 'I hope you don't either.'

The man purses his lips. 'I do,' he says.

Henry feels awkward about that. He hates talking to people in this class. He hates talking to people most of the time.

Yohan leans over. 'Is that what you didn't want me to ask?' he whispers. Henry won't respond.

The lecturer, Alice Oliver, looks like Woodstock, all scraggly, endlessly liberal. She's written COLOURLESS GREEN IDEAS SLEEP FURIOUSLY. What the heck is that?

'It's grammatically perfect,' she says. 'But of course, it's nonsense.'

This is insane. She says something else, something everyone seems to hear and understand. Henry doesn't get it. Maybe it's the accent thing again. It sounded like she said Ice Rink, just out of the blue. No one looked in any way confused. What does ice rink have to do with anything? Skating? Ice rink? A few moments after ice rink, she looks over at Henry, then around her, and begins talking again. I stink? But she wouldn't say I if she was talking about him. It doesn't make sense. That's nonsense. Okay, it's just paranoia taking hold. Could it have been more like English stink? The English stink? She could have been making a joke about him, given that the Irish like to make jokes about the English and given that he does actually stink. No one had laughed. Maybe they do really believe that English bastards stink?

The petrol stench is regrouping. It fills Henry's nose and begins to sear his throat. He feels he might be blushing but isn't sure. A warm zone is unwrapping from his neck to his cheeks. Clear the head, Henry. Clear the head and tune back in to the word of Alice Oliver, English expert. He knows he wants to think about the possibility that he's going to have a bit of an episode, but he won't allow it.

Alice Oliver is saying something about semantics. Six possible ways to jumble up verbs and nouns and adjectives to make a sentence structure fit for every language in the world. Too deep. No use. She ends her sentence. Then she says Gasoline. The class is silent. It was definitely Gasoline – Henry's sure of it.

Her next sentence begins. 'We've all heard about gang warfare, haven't we?'

The rest of the class seem locked onto her. Henry's starting to sweat. It might pour out of his face and dribble onto the desk. She writes SQUASHED INSECTS DON'T BITE MAD MENTAL RULE.

'Can you work it out?' she asks, grinning liberally, this time definitely not looking at Henry. His foot starts to bounce. He knows nothing about gang warfare and doesn't want any. His foot is making a noise. Things are going to start getting fast around here. He grips the new textbook on his desk, as if it offers some balance. Yohan glances over. Henry catches his eye. Yohan smiles, a knowing little grin. Henry looks away. What the hell is he doing with this book? What the fuck is he doing here? Why did he want to be a student in the first place, at this age, in this place? No use. No more. He puts the book into his duffle bag. He drops his pen in on top, and then his notebook. He's written *COLOURLESS GREEN IDEAS SLEEP FURIOUSLY* twice, at speed. He can't remember writing it at all.

'I need to get out,' he tells Yohan.

Alice smiles as he gets up and walks jelly-legged to the door. 'Don't you want to know about the Squashed Insects?'

Henry smiles again. 'No,' he says. It sounds indecent, but he leaves it the way it is. He exits.

There's not much to the corridor, but Henry can't wait to get out and into the fresh air. He walks fast, then sprints to and through the main door. Outside, he stops at a low wall in a green square and sits down. He puts his head between his knees, wishing he could vomit his sickness out of his body. Calm yourself down, Henry. Recognise it for what it is, accept it and calm down. Don't fight it, Henry. Go with it. That's the rule. That's what they tell you.

A cool wind picks up and makes the evening rustle and rush. Henry thinks about running into it, running the smell from his clothes and feeling the fresh air push into his face and down into his body. He could collect some of it and keep it, clean and crisp, inside him. Ever cool. God, I'm a wanker. God, he thinks, I'm twenty-six and still a wanker.

A man in a yellow jacket enters the lit, well-tended zone in which Henry now sits, his foot tapping bad Morse. A thick line of white glows across the man's chest. He's some kind of security guard who won't get knocked down. Henry looks up, telling himself not to make eye contact. He stares at the man. The man scans the building, noting which lights are on and which are off, ensuring the pattern is as it should be. He sees Henry staring and feels important. Henry looks away.

'Nice night,' he says, wondering if Henry has any right to be where he is.

Henry looks up, his fist tightening on his bag. 'Sorry,' he says.

He stands up urgently and walks off fast. The security guard thinks for a moment about following. He scans to see what Henry might have done. He spots a round omelette of vomit on the ground where he had been sitting. The man doesn't like that, but he's going to let it pass. Everyone's sick once in a while.

Yohan calls to him. 'You see a guy run through here?'

The man looks up from the vomit.

'A skinny fella,' Yohan clarifies.

'Aye,' says the security guard. 'He boked his ring here.'

Yohan wanders over to look. They both stare down at the

evidence. 'He does that the odd time,' Yohan says, and they both nod.

'Right,' says the man. 'Happens to the best of us.'

'Yep,' says Yohan.

Eight years ago, Henry Sender began to stop behaving like he needed a straitjacket. He started to slow down. Two years ago he came to Belfast, taking a job transfer no one wanted to a place where no one knew him. He had been able to bring his baggage and move into a rented flat alone. No one was going to expect or want anything from him there. He got annoyed by the city and its incestuous self-harming condition, but it was that which had made it fit for him in the first place. It ignored him and didn't get on with itself, and that was fine.

Now one of his foster mothers is on her deathbed. She's a kind woman. She's asked for Henry to be at her side, wanting to see his rosy cheeks, fine wavy dark hair and odd little ears before the ferocious cancer scaling through her core finally kills her. So far Henry hasn't even responded. The request was passed on to him by a woman in Social Services who knows how to connect foster kids with their old families.

Yohan had been surprised by Henry's attitude. He told him to get his arse to Newcastle upon Tyne and give the dying old dear a goodbye kiss. Yohan said if he didn't show, the old woman might hang on, pausing at the gates of the graveyard, waiting to see once again the oddest of the thirty-three children she had fostered. Henry didn't want to see her. He didn't want to revisit the past.

He'd explained it to Yohan over a pint after an aimless four-month night class at which they'd met. He'd said he wouldn't see her again, that he couldn't see her again. This, he had told his nosy friend, must mean that he didn't love her. He keeps thinking this. He's thinking it now. I don't love her. I don't care if she dies. He thinks about it all the time. So be it.

He buys sixty cigarettes on his way home. A headache begins as he walks away from the shop, three new bulges filling out his pockets. He tests himself. Do you want to die, Henry? No. Do you want to hide, Henry? Yes. To gorge yourself again on horrible whiskey and eat and smoke and sit up all night? No. Not really. Are you ashamed? Yes. Do you want to take a credit card and blitz it and own gold and art and ridiculous wines? Possibly. These questions and more tumble around in his head. The answers leave him feeling that he's really as fine as he could be. He's just had a bad reaction to the day. There's too much going on.

Henry has already met the man who will change his life, who will rewire his mind. The man will teach him something extraordinary and help his head balance more than it has ever balanced before. That man, Shuff Sheridan, is at this moment making an abusive phone call to a woman. Previously Shuff had intended to fix this woman to a wooden floor with one hundred six-inch nails. He had wanted to stake her down in an unmovable, bleeding metal block. He's explaining right now that he has wanted to do this to her in the past, and that he's done it before. He's giving her his name, address and number, just so she understands that he is completely serious about the things he says. But Shuff is also telling her that there has been a change of plan. He says he now intends to rip open her ribcage and stamp the air out of her lungs.

Henry goes home, calm and better, relaxed at the idea of relaxing. He's not a smoker, yet he smokes three cigarettes in a row, one from each packet, holding them away from his body in case he goes on fire. Dizzy as a scribble, laughing quietly, he sits on the toilet and empties his bowels, head in his hands, unable to remember if he has been sick, tasting something rich in his mouth. He wipes, and when he's sure there's no one near the front door of his little flat, he flushes. He washes and dries, goes into his bedroom, closes his curtains and snuggles up with himself and the faint smell of petrol.

He thinks about the device he forged in his head as a child. It didn't have a name, but it had an escape, a way out. It was a steel, barred mask. If he could, he would put it over his head now and lock it shut at the neck. He imagines lying there, the metal gripping tightly at his skull. He squeezes his eyes together and thinks about his stupid fears, about providing the Pisser, getting shot with petrol, the lecture hall, the students, the lecturer and the security guard. He thinks mostly about that poor white-haired old woman, waiting, holding onto her life and praying for the brief return of that troubled little boy. Henry goes foetal, his head loud with echoes, and tries to focus only on that mask, on the way it can fix things forever. It has a short, fat revolver welded into its side, lined up directly with the centre of his brain. He would rest his palm on the handle, his index finger on the trigger. Again, he has his fleeting thought of suicide. Again, he knows that's all a suicidal thought needs to be. He won't admit it to anyone, but he'd love to just pull that thing and call it a day.

Back to Shuff Sheridan: Henry's mate Yohan had been talking about Shuff in the pub a couple of weeks ago, and not for the first time. He'd told Henry a fresh bunch of things about Shuff, adoring him in the way straight men adore heroes. Henry wasn't really interested.

Yohan? Not important. But thirty, Belfast, unhappily married, enjoys secretarial-style sex lines and middle-ranking misery in others. On paper, he's a big-hearted volunteer, helping violent ex-prisoners resettle into the community. In action, he's a man in awe of the thug, a once-bullied weakling who wishes he could join the ranks of the bully and wreak bully havoc. Yohan spends a lot of time getting to know his clients, calling at their homes to see what they need, to hear what they'll tell him, to see if they'll answer things he shouldn't ask, things about violence and rage and revenge. He's tasked by charity with working out their needs for the rocky, unlocked road ahead. Sometimes they fascinate him, sometimes they ruin his day with a story or a punch, sometimes they prove they'd been taken apart and never rebuilt. Yohan enjoys it all.

Shuff Sheridan is one of these former prisoners, back on the streets for a year now after four in the clink for battering an old man, for wiping his memory with his fists. Yohan thinks Shuff is the real steel deal and has never been so in awe of anyone in his life.

3

It's pitch black when he awakes, but after a time his old eyes adjust. There's a single shaft of sunlight, angled towards a sky he can't see, lasering in from a penny-size hole above and to his left. It illuminates black walls but sheds no light on his situation. He's lying down, feet bare, clothed only from the waist up. It's cold and damp and cramped.

Francis M.N. Cleary is confused, but that's nothing new. By way of example, just last week, dressed in pyjamas, he walked out of the nursing home, babbling something about losing a door. Three weeks ago, for most of a day, he said he was sure he was in France, and possibly a Frenchman. He threw an onion at the communal television. Many of the staff at the nursing home can't stand him. Sometimes he's just too much work.

Frank reasons that he might have been locked away somewhere by a nurse who has had enough of him. He considers too that he may have been kidnapped and imprisoned as a penalty for some previous crime. But, after a time, he feels it's likely that he has found a large metal box somewhere and climbed into it. He can't be sure. He can't remember. He's ninety-one and his mind has become overcrowded.

Night begins to fall and dogs bark and Francis remains damp, uncomfortable and caged in a small, smelly space that may or may not be in or around the nursing home.

With so little to go on Francis, who wears only a threadbare, blue and white striped pyjama top, knows he has to get some facts. Reaching up with one hand, he feels the cold surface of his ceiling. It's as greasy a thing as could be. He rubs his hands together and now feels a thick, gooey, grimy, gritty film between them. His arm hurts as he feels to his left and right, to where the walls meet the ceiling. He decides that the shape of this place is oblong. Above his chest is a line that runs the width of his ceiling, an overlapping edge of steel. It serves no obvious purpose from the inside.

His sagged muscles on their light bones aren't strong enough to knock the steel to any meaningful degree. When he tries, he gets a dull tap from the greasy surface, but it doesn't tell him anything. He pushes on the walls around him, but nothing moves.

Breathing in deeply, Francis tries to sense more. There are overlapping odours, he decides in time, all of which he's smelled before. But, as so often happens with so many things these days, he can't recall what they are. Running his hands along the floor, he feels that it's as if he's partly lying in a sludge pool of some kind. It's slimy, thick at the bottom, peppered with small bits and pieces of matter. As he tilts his old neck to either side, he feels a cold, foreign goop caress him. His whole body seems to be lying in some kind of revolting, near empty bath. He wonders if it is some kind of torture, and considers that this is not necessarily a bad thing.

His left hand touches something tougher than the other bits of lodged stuff. It's thin, firm and long, like a strap but not attached to anything. He tries to grasp it, although his motor functions are weak. After a minute, he manages to lift it to his nose, and a part of it, a piece of metal, flops onto his face. Again, this smell is familiar. Is this somewhere he has been before? He takes another whiff. The image of a dog flashes through his mind, but he doesn't know why. He tries again to focus. For the best part of the next five minutes he continues to smell that old leather dog collar without knowing what it is.

Police had, some hours earlier, arrived at the nursing home. Francis M.N. Cleary had been absent for eleven hours and fifteen minutes and there had been no sightings. One nurse – she calls herself Rhonda because she prefers it to Rita – had a guilty secret about it all, but was keeping mum. Rhonda knew that a man with a funny run had thrown Frank, dressed only in his pyjama top, over his shoulder, climbed out of a window and made off through the field at the back of the nursing home. The problem was that the man – he'd appeared from under the bed while Rhonda was nipping, witchlike, at Frank's weak ankles – had pushed her head hard up against a wall. He had told her that if she was ever able to describe the man she was looking at, then that man would come back and kill her. Oddly enough, Rhonda was okay with that. She'd been frightened, but she knew she'd cooperate with police if it came to the point where Frank seemed to have gone for good. She had morals, even though her heart kicked with excitement when she nipped at the ankles of the elderly, particularly the ones whom no one visited.

But then the man had stared into her in dead silence as she gasped behind the hard surface of his palm. He stared and stared, not blinking, not moving. He stared and stared and then, with his free hand, gently reached into his pocket and removed a bunch of keys. He selected the longest – a particularly jagged silver affair – and brought it close to her face. He pulled the skin back above one eye, forbidding its closure. He brought the key closer and Rhonda felt a searing terror run through her, sole to soul. He caught the edge of a contact lens with the edge of that jagged key and slid it, ever so carefully, across that trembling eye. Rhonda's vision blurred and her bladder weakened.

The man released her, pulled back, threw the waiting, confused Francis over his shoulder, climbed out of the window, keys in hand, and ran off, jingling, with an unusual gait. Rhonda was left frozen against the wall, shivering and urinating gently, a red blotch accenting her forehead. The man had chilled her to her core in those moments. She had never known such horror. She felt he had somehow snatched, from the certain privacy of her mind, information on the one thing that terrified her above all: blindness. He would be back to blind her if she said anything. And to that end, Rhonda's secret about the disappearance of Francis M.N. Cleary was as secure as the Gates of Hell.

An uninterested policeman had gathered some details about old Frank from staff. He secured a description ('his eyes are blue, Constable, but the whites are yellow'), some details about the state of his physical health ('his mental health is the main problem, Constable'), and what he was last known to be wearing ('his pyjamas, Constable, to the best of my knowledge'). A duty manager also relayed some of Frank's previous flirtations with freedom, but said she couldn't believe he had the strength to secure an effective escape alone. This seemed to be a worrying situation, she said.

Some time later, a gossiping cook sidled up to the policeman and told a lie. She said she too knew old Frank and that she would be happy to answer questions.

The officer asked one: 'Do you know him well?'

'Yes,' she said. 'Like the back of my hand.'

'Any ideas where he might be?'

She paused. 'No,' she said.

'Do you really know him well?'

'No,' she said. 'I knew him a bit.'

'Right,' he said. 'I probably know him better than you.'

'Oh,' she said, momentarily holding the O shape on her lips, her eyebrows raised and awaiting his expansion.

'You don't know him at all, do you?'

'No,' she said. 'But I heard he was a fireman.'

The policeman smiled. 'Not quite. But that's a good one.'

'Is it?' she asked. 'Why? What was he?'

'He wasn't a fireman.'

'What was he?'

'He was the kind of guy who said he started fires, but he wasn't a fireman.'

'Was he one of them arsonists?'

'No, love. Look,' he glanced around, bored with the woman, thinking of leaving. 'He was in the paper and all. I'm surprised you haven't heard of him.'

The O shape appeared again, then: 'What was he in the paper for?'

'For being nuts,' he said.

'Nuts?'

'Yep. He's a fantasist.'

'Oh.' A pregnant pause, a beating heart. 'What do you mean?'

'He confesses to crimes all the time. Well, he did before he ended up in here.'

'Oh,' she said. 'Now, I didn't know that.'

'Right,' said the policeman. 'Well, now you do.'

'Yes,' she said, her lively eyes holding onto him, eyebrows raised again.

'He wrote a book, some wacky philosophy stuff. Ended up teaching it at the university. They threw him out.'

'Philosophy? Jesus wept. So why did they throw him out of the university?'

'Because he said he had set fire to a church.' A pause. 'Like a fireman would.'

'Oh.' She held the shape again.

'He hadn't, by the way. He also said he stole a fire engine, beat up some people, stole some cars, nailed a woman to a

floor. He's crackers, love.'
'Jesus. I didn't know that.'
'Well, there you go. We call him Frank the Fess.'
'Frank the Fess?'
'Aye.'
'Oh.'
'As in confessor.'
'Ah. And there was me thinking he was a fireman.'
'Right. Well, you didn't know him that well, to be fair.'
'Aye,' she said. 'I didn't know him at all, to be fair.'

My dear old friend,

I have considered giving them a name. I have thought and thought and been so close to picking up the phone with that name. And now, after all this time, I have finally done it. It has begun. It has started. I have given them a name.

I wrote it down and sent it to a Detective Sergeant John Ryan. I told him that Francis M.N. Cleary had killed the woman, that if he looked into the crime he would find that I was behind it. She died last week. She had been nailed to a wooden floor in her own front room. My God. The police said it took her some considerable time to die. I have been imagining the scene and I am disturbed by what I can picture. Her murder was the last straw.

Detective Sergeant Ryan rang me and said I had made a mistake. I said I hadn't. I said I had killed her. He told me to Get a Life. I told him he should get a new expression. He didn't understand. He doesn't understand.

Regards, old friend,

Francis Cleary

4

GADAKA   Hello. You look pretty.
LILBIT   Hi baby.
JOBO   HEY SEXY!!!!!!!!
GRANT   Hi
BIGNUTS How much hunny??
JOBO $$$???
MUSCLES here kitty kittyyyyyyy
GRANT   You show tits now baby???
LILBIT   Not now. in private. Hi jobo hi grant.
BIGNUTS Hey hi 2me?
JOBO   Mmmmm u so horny.
LILBIT   Hi big. Hi muscle
GRANT   Show titties then we go pvt.
BIGNUTS Awww. Have you been a bad girl?
LILBIT   Only in pvt grant. Yes big;–)
MUSCLES Muscles
JOBO   How much????????
LILBIT   1.99 baby
BIGNUTS yummmm. U like lollipops?
GADAKA   I'm coming into private, Lilbit.
LILBIT   yes big. Hi gad. great xxxx.
MUSCLES show dat asssssssssssssssss

GADAKA   Hello.
LILBIT   hi baby!!!! Welcom in my room!!!!
GADAKA   Don't they drive you mad?

LILBIT	No baby they ok. Just horny guys! Mmmmm its cooool xx
GADAKA	That doesn't mean they can forget their manners.
LILBIT	You sweet! xx
GADAKA	They're scum. All of them. You look amazing. Sit forward.
LILBIT	it better?
GADAKA	Very nice. Why so cheap? You look like a 2.99, or more, to me.
LILBIT	Aw thanks baby. 1.99 keeps lilbit busy.
GADAKA	You would always be busy. You should charge more and perhaps sleep more.
LILBIT	I like job. xx
GADAKA	No. That's a lie.
LILBIT	Hahahahaha!!!! Its ok. Not 4ever but its best 4 me now:−)
GADAKA	What age are you?
LILBIT	18 4 real. What age u like baby?
GADAKA	Eighteen is good for now.
LILBIT	What age u?
GADAKA	Average. Where do you live?
LILBIT	Who cares baby xxx u like kiss me?
GADAKA	What city?
LILBIT	I don't like say that. Not matters
GADAKA	I want you to tell me, or I'll go.
LILBIT	no don't go baby. Ok don't laugh
GADAKA	Why would I laugh?
LILBIT	what city u in?
GADAKA	Why would I laugh?
LILBIT	I live iasi in rumania
GADAKA	I know where it is. North east, university town. There's a saint in a church there.

LILBIT	hey yes baby! St Parascheva!! She my protector!!!! Where u?
GADAKA	That's irrelevant. Why would I have laughed?
LILBIT	Rumania. People say bad things. Baggars, vampires etc!!!
GADAKA	I don't. I love countries like Romania.
LILBIT	Cool xxx u love lilbit too????
GADAKA	I love countries where everything that works is about to break.
LILBIT	xxxx
GADAKA	You make me smile, Lilbit. Perform for me.
LILBIT	What you like see baby?
GADAKA	You. I want you to unfold.
LILBIT	You want strip honey?? See what under lilbit panties?
GADAKA	Naturally.
LILBIT	xxxxxxx u wan see????!!! xx
GADAKA	Yes I do. Do the things you might expect me to ask for. Do what you think I might like.
LILBIT	that a lot things my baby!!!
GADAKA	I can leave if you don't want to.
LILBIT	No baby that cool don't go xxxx
GADAKA	Thank you. Tell me your name.
LILBIT	u call me lilbit babt
GADAKA	Tell me your real name.
LILBIT	Alina. U say aleeena like this xx
GADAKA	Nice. I won't type as I watch you and I will leave when I'm finished with you.
LILBIT	xx
GAKADA	I will come back to you another time, sweet Alina, if you're good. Money is no object.
LILBIT	Cool baby u the best xx
GADAKA	Play.
LILBIT	ok u wathc lilbit play now baby xx

5

They're less than two minutes into the flight from Belfast to London when Shuff Sheridan dials a number on his mobile phone. He wants to remind Maggie, his wife, to tell callers to the door to go and fuck themselves while he's out of the country. To his immediate left sits young Henry Sender, staring into an in-flight magazine, panicked to the chromosomes that Shuff's illicit call will bring unwelcome official attention. Worse, ish, that it'll make the plane crash and kill everyone.

Says Shuff, after dispensing his husbandly advice: 'Awlabest love.'

Shuff ends the call and turns to Henry. He wonders if Henry's aware there's an angry red spot brewing on the side of his nose.

'What're you reading about?' he asks.

'Ah, some crap about cheese.' Henry hopes he'll soon feel less nervous when talking to Shuff.

'Right,' says Shuff. 'Cheese is dead on.' A pause. 'So you think me ringing someone on the mobile will make the plane crash?'

Henry's stomach lurches upwards. 'What? No, no.' A pause. 'Well, possibly.'

'Lemme tell you, Henry, lad. If a fucken phone could make this thing crash and kill two hundred people in one pop, d'you not think they'd take them off you at the door?'

'Well, they're pretty strict about turning them off.' Henry

doesn't want to have this conversation. Switching phones off on planes is not a rule he came up with, nor one he wants to enforce. Shuff can ring anyone he likes.

Says Shuff: 'So if we leave them on, we'll crash? Me arse. Tell that to them Muslims. "Abdullah, leave yer phone on and crash the plane."'

'They say they interfere with the systems, or something.'

Shuff flicks his eyes up. 'What does that mean? Fucken nothing. Interferes with systems. Fuck's sake.'

'The signal can get pulled through the, you know, machines in the cockpit. Something like that.'

Shuff scrunches up his face. 'You think the captain was picking up me and the wife chattin?'

'No. They say it could make instruments give the wrong readings or something. I don't know.'

'Ack, the back of me arse.' A pause. 'I love that blue cheese, so I do. Stilton. You know it?'

'Yes.' Henry hopes this sharp turn will mean the phone conversation is over. It's already taken years off his life. Cheese is less controversial. 'It's very tasty.'

'Aye. I eat an awful fucken lot of it, so I do.'

'That right?'

'Aye. I've got me own shelf in the fridge.'

'Just for Stilton? Wow.'

'Aye.' A pause. 'Well, no. For cheese. All types.'

'Nice one.'

'Aye. Wife hates the fucken smell of it, so she does.'

'Yes. I can understand that.'

'She says it's like rotten socks.'

'I see.'

'Fucks her right up.'

'Right.'

Shuff leans a little closer: 'It interferes with her systems.'

'Very funny.'
'Aye.'

It's three months since Henry first heard about Shuff, and he's known him for just over a week. He was there one night when Yohan asked Henry out for a pint in a dead bar. Henry knew that the wide and blue-eyed stranger was the allegedly magnificent and fearless Shuff as soon as he saw him. Shuff was drinking neat vodka with one hand, fixing his crotch with the other and constantly eyeing everyone in the bar. Henry thought Shuff was avoiding eye contact with him. He thought it was a bit pathetic. Shuff wasn't. Truth is, he had Henry sussed straight away and was looking elsewhere for other information about nothing in particular. Henry had been a shade bugged by the fact that Shuff's forty-four-year-old legs stayed wide apart all night, as if forcing himself to suggest he had the biggest balls and was therefore, under some atavistic code, the top dog among the trio. Henry had misread that one too, as it turned out.

Yohan introduced Shuff as one of his clients. Henry had half-expected his English bones to be ground when he shook Shuff's heavy hand, but he was wrong. He couldn't work out if the relatively weak handshake meant Shuff was insincere or just not pushed about the macho handshake codes which Henry had been screwing up his entire life. Nonetheless he judged him initially on his handshake, deciding Shuff was probably all talk, that inside he probably wasn't really much of a man at all. Ex-prisoner, he thought. They must talk a lot of shit, and Yohan's job is to lap it up. Bark, bark – no bite.

It was on that night that the idea of Shuff going to Romania with Henry was born. Yohan knew too much about Henry's little frets and fears, and said too much about them when he was drinking. Yes, Henry had been diagnosed with bipolar disorder when he was just eight. His cyclic condition would pitch his head against itself, compelling him to live in the contrast between deathly, still fear and then a sudden, unstoppable blur of raging, sometimes joyous, life. Manic, then depressive. Manic. Depressive.

He'd frequently wanted to die fast, live faster, drink everything, eat himself, lie, suffer, cut his hair off and shrink with shame. He'd often climbed into or under his bed and lain still for silent hours, genuinely hoping the world would be hit by a giant meteorite. And he'd always feared he was about to get beaten up and stabbed because he was a forever foreign sort of guy to most people.

And it got worse in his teens. Then he would have episodes which led those who cared for this orphan to believe they had surely done something wrong, that they were driving him insane. But all things change. Henry's condition has pretty much stabilised now, as is the fickle nature of that cranial coin. His chemical imbalance all but managed itself, slowly reducing the headspins as it released the child, the adolescent, into the safer, more balanced grip of adulthood. Therapy too had helped beat back the illness, and age and complex combinations of drugs had mopped up most of its residue. Yes, Henry was still able to surprise himself, scare himself, living under the tricky rule of this thing's remaining wit. And yes, Yohan understood it. But Yohan liked to play with it, to use it as a way to manipulate friendship, to try and involve himself further in Henry's life by using his understanding of his past. It was invasive and rude, even though Yohan did know what Henry needed sometimes. He was a good judge of character in that way.

Yohan knew that Henry was planning to go to Romania for a very brief trip, and that his biggest fear was of being attacked, stabbed or murdered over there. It was a rock solid fear of the unknown, of how he would react to it, of who could help out if he lost the plot and hit, once again, that cerebral throttle. Henry had built himself a stability in Belfast, and yet here he was planning to take a risk he wasn't sure he could so much as calculate. Yohan understood that this potential trip was brave, and considered it an excellent idea. He also considered it an excellent opportunity for him to pair Henry up with a man who might just show him how thrilling life can be.

Did Henry want what Yohan called a One Man Army at his side, a proven, fearless, loyal heavy, paid to defend him during dodgy business away out there in Romania? Yes. That would be helpful, given that Henry would be in charge. But aside from what Yohan had waxed lyrical about, Henry didn't know anything about Shuff, and now he wasn't sure he was this One Man Army just because he sat with his legs too far apart, molested his own groin and took strangers by surprise with his handshake. Indeed, the more he learned about Shuff, the more he feared he was some kind of psycho.

Henry debated the idea with himself that night in the dead bar as Yohan and Shuff talked at length about savoury foodstuffs and a history of violence. He asked his instincts what they honestly said. They said yes, but still Henry was minded to say no. The more he heard bits of conversation about the kind of things Shuff had got up to, beyond making enormous sandwiches, the more he began to fear that Shuff might indeed be a One Man Army. If so, wasn't he more likely to attract violence, or even start violence, in Romania than he would if he wasn't a One Man Army? After a while, Henry stopped listening to himself altogether, but when he came back round he couldn't remember whether he wanted Shuff to go with him or not.

When he was asked directly, he didn't want to appear as if Shuff's presence or absence really meant much to him. He tried to show that he wasn't as much of a coward as Yohan had probably said he was. So Henry said that the idea was probably cool, if Shuff wanted to. They all said they'd think about it, and Henry was glad. He thought the whole thing might get lost during the night, and he thought about doing the same himself. But Shuff went to the toilet a short while later and when he returned, zipping his flies in the bar, he announced that he was going to Romania.

'Me granda was Russian,' he told them, sitting down with a thump and spreading his heavy thighs. 'Communist as fuck, so he was.'

Yohan was delighted with Shuff's news. He enjoyed the certain thought that it was too late for Henry to call it off now.

Earlier that day, Henry had walked around Ormeau Park for the best part of an hour, weighing up the options for the coming days. He had slipped into a clump of bushes and sat down, hidden from view and unable to see anyone, his back to a stout trunk with *Anarchy* and *Fat* carved into it. It was in there that he thought again about how strange he was because he didn't love his former foster mother, even in what must be her final days. He decided he must now accept that and go, not to her, but east instead. It was one way or the other. He had to go somewhere, to address one of his issues. He couldn't just do nothing. Going to Eastern Europe could reap a rich reward, and though he considered the risk to be higher, it was surely the best thing for him to do if he was serious about holding onto the website. Although, if he was honest with himself, he couldn't pretend that business matters were at the front of his mind.

Adrian Harrison had left a shocking mess when he croaked after a lifted, loaded skip fell on him ten months ago – and not just a mess on the ground. A forensic audit exposed nearly half a million pounds worth of dodgy dealing and investments that left his wife, Lizzie, unable to sleep. He had poured thousands into a new hotel in Phuket, Thailand, which would become noted for its discretion, and yet more into travelling to it. He had bought an expansive flat in that part of Moldova most sympathetic to the West, and had taken pictures of the teenage girls he had paid to decorate it. And he had married a Chinese peasant girl in Beijing, later flying her to that European flat and keeping her in the manner to which she was accustomed. He had other young girls move in too, and even managed to arrange for a local man to collect rent from them once a month. Soon men from the West began calling at the door, and the girls became prostitutes in no time. The rent went up.

Lizzie, who felt like a right prick after learning all this, always thought Adrian had been touring the golf courses of the world. She rang his friend Noel to ask him had they ever played golf on their regular vacations and Noel just said: 'Look, Adie liked young girls. Cute foreign things. It's no big deal.'

Lizzie, her son Michael, and daughter Amy decided to sell off what they could, and to ditch what they couldn't. The website would be the first thing to go. It was legal, but it wasn't the sort of thing they wanted the family name linked with. One morning Lizzie suggested passing it on to Henry, that strange little eleven-year-old they had fostered for two unusual years. Henry, Lizzie reminded her unsure offspring, had always liked to sit in darkened wardrobes with pieces of old radios and pretend he was controlling destiny via some kind of computer. He'd liked to steal knives and bulbs and food, and to vomit and then dwell in hedges, in lonely little societies of his own creation. When he was calm, he watched television programmes about computers, made little beeps to himself and spoke, wide-eyed, of the powerful networks which linked nation to nation, friend to friend, foe to foe.

The Harrisons had always liked the lad, although they never saw much of him. But they'd missed analysing his absences after he moved on to the home of a new foster mother, a woman who is now dying. They didn't know what had become of him.

The siblings agreed that what had surely been a burgeoning interest in computers had probably escalated, and amid a nostalgic chat, they said yes, okay, let's give the little guy a little high-tech cut of what was left of Adrian Harrison and move on.

Through Social Services, Henry learned that a former foster father had left him his internet business. It was a website called Woundlicker Dot Com, and in a short letter Lizzie said she had, being old and unfashionable, no idea what it was. She said it was making some money and that Henry, being a young and presumably trendy, web-literate guy, would probably know what to do with it. She wished him well and left no return address. As to the rest of the discoveries – including the discreet hotel, the mortgage-free, money-making Moldovan flat – the dividends just kept rolling in and, with the help of Adrian's discreet accountant, the Harrisons soon got over their blushes.

The solicitor who handled Henry's inheritance was uncomfortable with the conversation. He said the business was making just under a couple of grand a month in profit. He said it was managed by a company called QuestorCyber in the Netherlands, who seemed to have an excellent reputation. Henry's only responsibilities would be to decide the general direction of the business and deal with issues raised by clients, as long as they weren't technical. Technical operation was all down to QuestorCyber. It was a long time before the solicitor stopped talking and shuffling papers and paused, as if cueing Henry to ask the question.

'What type of internet business is it?'

The solicitor laughed. He looked up and bobbed his head from side to side and smiled a false smile.

'Chat hosting,' he said, pushing a piece of paper over to Henry's side of the table. It was something printed from a computer screen. Twelve pictures of girls posing, a dozen states of undress, ten dozen fantasies. Yet it was the faces which caught and held Henry's eye, which doubled the knot in his stomach. The faces pouted, offered, watched, stared, stunned, beckoned, provoked, absorbed and more. Henry knew this was the most alarming piece of A4 he'd ever seen.

'Wow,' was the word which slipped from his mouth.

'I know,' said the solicitor. 'Most people are only left a bit of a house.'

Henry went home that day with his mind in a muddle. He sat down with a coffee at his computer, logged on and keyed in the address Woundlicker Dot Com. A royal blue background surfaced into frame, a bold yellow title scrolled itself along the top of the page and twelve little squares popped open one by one. There, like an alternative Advent calendar, were the photographs of his girls, each with looks set to stun, with underwear a hot second from revelation. Twelve on the page, and six pages of twelve.

'Wow,' he said again.

He rolled his mouse around, running the cursor over the divine outlines, and clicked on someone called WILDLOVER. A new window sprung obediently open, the borders of two larger square boxes were drawn, fast line by fast line, and WILDLOVER's live image appeared on the left hand side of his computer screen. She was lying, front down, on a bed, head in her hands, healthy long blonde hair combed back, a dildo at her side, eighteen-year-old hazel eyes flicking, glinting from the white light of the words eagerly typed into a free chatroom by men with real names they wouldn't use. She wore a black thong, its string disappearing into the perfectly curved dark line between her clean, compact buttocks, and a black tube top which cut across the bright whiteness of her back like a censor's rule. Occasionally, playfully, she flicked up a leg or two, signalling that she was lots of fun but lazy too. Occasionally she smiled at some of the lies paraded before her by husbands in offices, hotels and studies around the planet. All WILDLOVER wanted them to do was leave the free chatroom, click on the private link and begin a one-on-one session during which she would do as she was asked. It would, as always, end in the minute-to-minute debiting of credits at one end, and a guilty little orgasm at the other.

Henry clicked on the door of the free chatroom to allow him to enter and see what was being said. It asked him for a name. He wrote LOP. They were the three letters closest to his right hand. Seconds later, LOP was stacked at the bottom of a list of fourteen other easy, false names. Most of them were asking things like *will you fuck ass with dildo baby?* and *show me pussy then we go private$$$????*. A few minutes passed before WILDLOVER's image disappeared. A stock message replaced the place where she had been:

> 'Model is in private;–) Why not buy credits and hang on – she'll be back soon!'

Henry hung on. Six minutes later and the words vanished. WILDLOVER appeared back on the screen, fixing her pants and hair before lying back down on her front again. She lifted a white teddy bear, which had made its way to front of camera, and put it out of view. She pressed a button on her keyboard and gave a cute smile.

hi guys, she wrote, *wildlover sooooo horny*.

Henry pressed his cursor onto a little square which read:

Click here to talk privately with this model.

Another window appeared.

To talk privately with WILDLOVER you have to become a member of Woundlicker Dot Com and buy credits. It's free to join!

WILDLOVER charges $2.99 per minute. If you are a member, please enter your password below and continue. If not, just sign up here!★

In less than one minute you can be one-on-one in WILDLOVER's private room!'

★All details are held securely by QuestorCyber – hosts can only know who you are if you tell them!

Henry thought he wouldn't join his own website. He was too afraid of revealing who he might be, too scared of what he might do to himself in front of the live image of a dirt-poor Ukrainian teenager.

Shuff asks Henry to let him out. 'I need a piss,' he explains.

Henry stands in the aisle as Shuff lifts all five feet eleven inches of his frame, evidently feeling the weight of his own body. It's not that Shuff's fat or particularly unfit, it's more that he looks like he's overworked, perhaps a little tired. Henry thinks that his broad body has given a lot in its lifetime, that it's breaking, that it has broken things. To look at him, or even listen to him, you'd expect Shuff would be the kind of guy who had built up a sizeable beer belly, but that's not the case. He has one, but it's the belly of a man in his thirties, not forties. It's the belly of someone whose muscles are only just beginning to really surrender. His skin is leathery and he shaves badly, leaving thick patches of black hair like a worn-out brush on the rounded curves of his face. It's as if his features are concentrated in the centre, flanked by semi–tennis ball, almost amusing cheeks. His hair is dark yard brush, short, uneven (self-cut?), standing up, black and thick. It's grey around the edges, but it's the hard darkness that stands out. For the third or fourth time, as Shuff slides his way out to the aisle, Henry catches sight of the tattoos under the older man's sleeves. He can't make out what they are, but he can see swirls of small capital letters encircling his forearms. He sees ENIERP. They're determined arms which, Henry thinks, belie their strength. Not too broad, ill-defined, but muscular. There's just a hint of flab. All in all, Henry thinks, Shuff Sheridan looks bigger than he is.

Henry sits back down and picks at the netted seat pocket in front of him. ENIERP? No idea. He reminds himself to keep his mind made up that he has chosen correctly. Henry's trying to be collected, to look on all of this as an adventure, telling himself he has to keep the spirit of adventure to the fore, to untie the ship and sail away from the safe harbour. This is a pioneering and personally defining voyage and Shuff is now part of whatever it will bring. Henry feels suddenly as if he may vomit, and his brain is ram-raided by footage of him filling his sick bag and flinging it, open-necked, along the plane. What would people say? What could they do to him up here? His foot starts to bounce. But there will be no mania, only the memory of it. Besides, he's taken a just-in-case pill just in case, and he has faith that it will be enough.

He sees Shuff's phone tucked into the netting of his vacated seat. Does he have the nerve to switch it off? Nope. Please

God, he thinks, his lips moving and a hand checking for sweat on his forehead, don't let this man make another phone call. Please do not let his phone ring.

When Henry had signed all the papers and the transaction was complete, he became the webmaster for Woundlicker Dot Com. He liked the title. A package of forms was forwarded and, after ringing QuestorCyber, he was able to reset the late Adrian Harrison's password – it had been KINGOF GOLF. A little tally in the top corner of the screen blurred and stopped on the number 43. There were emails from QuestorCyber, from current chat hosts and from girls who wanted to become them. QuestorCyber was dropping him statistics outlining site traffic in terms of minutes per month and mapping out which girls had been online and for how long in the previous four weeks. Someone called Eric Z explained how the central server – the largely self-reliant operating system which managed all the traffic – had been upgraded and now had more bandwidth than ever. He told Henry, whom they referred to as *Adrain*, that this should iron out most of the image delays and make the hosts look as live as ever. They reminded him he was with the most up-and-coming video-chat software firm on the market. Eric Z signed off saying: 'Let's stay recession-proof together!'

The emails from the girls were much easier to understand.

> Helo Adrian and hi, my name is Ecaterina. I am from in Bucharest in Rumania and I am now 18 year of ages. Please could you email to me the form to fill as I am would like to be a chat host on the wonderful woundlicker website:–) My picture you will see has a good body and cloths. I am like to work many hours and I am like meeting guys from the world. No I am

> not a professional but I am can do a good job. Email me
> soon please and I am will email the details on the page
> and etcs. You have my picture attach and I am would
> like to use epassporte for ID proof which is the best.
> Thank you sir, Ecaterina.

Eventually, after downing two fizzy drinks and listening to the radio at full volume for the guts of an hour, Henry wrote:

> Dear Ecaterina. Attached is the form you requested.
> Thank you for your interest. I'm sorry it has taken so
> long for this to get to you, but the site has changed
> hands and I'm just finding out how it all works. I'm a
> webmaster! And great pic by the way!! Henry.

> Hi Adrian. You say limit is 3.99 but why can I not go
> 4.99? I can get it as have many regs who stay for long
> times:–) Please talk with me to fix this or maybe I find
> other place to let me for 4.99? Sabina xx

After half an hour in the toilet, both his head and arse threatening imminent release, Henry replied:

> Dear Sabina. Thanks for your enquiry. The site has
> recently changed hands and Adrian is no longer the
> webmaster. My name's Henry and I am the webmaster.
> Forgive me for the late reply, it's just that I'm still trying
> to learn all about it as I have no experience in this
> business. I can't see any reason why you shouldn't
> charge what you like. It's supply and demand after all! I
> have emailed QuestorCyber and asked them how I can
> get rid of Adrian's bar on the site which won't allow
> models to charge more than 3.99. The 60/40 percentage
> cut is also under review. I'm sure QuestorCyber will get
> back to me soon. I will email you again when it's been

sorted out. I hope all this makes sense. Oh and I love your pix! Henry.

Hello Ad man. You have made a mistake:–(The girl using my camera was me and you have my epassporte copy so you know I am 18. I don't know who told you anything if it was mens or others but the girl they talk about was not on my account. Its might be other chat hosts who want me in trouble. It is only me uses this. If some girl says she is 14 she is not on my cam. Only I Selda use my cam and I have no others who do work. That is my answer to you. Are you coming to meet with me as the way you said? Xx

After ten minutes of looking at her picture, and four of flossing his teeth to bloody perfection, Henry wrote:

Dear Selda. My name's Henry and I have recently taken over the site from Adrian. I have checked through his emails to get to the bottom of this matter and have found that he was contacted by one concerned customer who said that a girl who claimed she was 14 was working from your account. I don't know if this happened or not. I hope not. All I can say is that I will be carefully monitoring events from now on. No one under 18 is allowed to perform, or use this website at all. This is a clear moral and legal issue and if I discover that it has happened, I will have no choice but to have you ejected. It is also possible to have your epassporte blacklisted. That's all I can say on the matter. I presume the invitation to Adrian was personal, so I can only tell you that he will not be able to meet with you. I'm sorry. Best regards, Henry. Oh and I love your pix!!

> My dears Adrian. My name is Alina. I have been working for your website for six months since I turn 18. I enjoy it very much and I thank you for your good rate to giving me 60 percent. Excuse me but I have notice that there is advertisements for your website as customers have pressed them and landed on woundlicker dot com. They have told me in chatroom that is my picture being used in this advertisements and I have looked and I see this is very true. It is one of the pictures I use on my profile page which I take with my webcam. Excuse me but I am wonder from you if it is possible to get something for this because is extra to what is in your kind contract? I am not fighting not want to bother you but I like to ask as I would be great helped by any other money to me. I am sorry. Alina.

After three minutes of admiring her image, and three eating a sandwich, Henry responded:

> Dear Alina. My name is Henry and I have recently taken over the site from Adrian. I can only apologise that your picture has been used without your consent. I have arranged for QuestorCyber to put an extra $100 into your account this month and you will be able to withdraw it via your epassporte card in the usual way. Should you permit the further use of the picture, I propose to do the same each month, mainly because I can't imagine a better one! Please let me know if this is okay, or if you would instead like me to have the picture removed. Best regards, Henry. PS: You look a million dollars Alina!

That was all eight weeks ago. In time, Henry got round to answering every email and began to enjoy what he was doing. It was dead simple really. The girls appeared to find him fine to deal with and he tried to stay as professional as possible, soon deciding not to end each missive with a wolf whistle. He didn't have to see anyone, go anywhere or talk to anyone in meetings like a businessman. He just had to sit in his flat, unknown, and type professional-sounding words that helped the thing tick along. In one way he thought the service to be charitable, spreading a slither of wealth from the West to the East in exchange for services which did not involve the girls having to touch anyone. He soon packed in his job at the call centre – taking frustrating, hard-to-hear calls from people reporting problems with their phones – and decided to do only this. It paid better, it was legal, it gave him acres of directionless time, and it gave him a kick.

Selda replied a few days later, thanking him for not booting her off the website and explained that Adrian had phoned her once, telling her that he was going to pay a visit to his best chat hosts on a trip to Romania and the Ukraine. He had explained it would be a business trip but that he was bringing some goods which could help the hosts in their trade. The goods would have included new outfits, including a PVC bodysuit which Adrian had planned to present to Selda before attempting to screw her senseless, but only Adrian ever knew that. Wily Selda, suspecting that there might have been some money involved in such a visit, suggested that Henry might want to consider the same thing? Henry said he wanted to learn a little more about the business first, but that he would think on it. He suspected, of course, that paying a visit to a cooperative Selda might end up with him parting with money and clothing and having a joyous romp with her. But he also suspected that it might end up with him being cornered by half a dozen Romanian hard men who would relieve him of his cash and teeth and stick long knives into his thin body.

Selda would, of course, know nothing at all about such a violent turn of events. What faith could he have in a girl who may well have been prostituting a fourteen-year-old on the internet?

Alina had replied very positively, thanking Henry profusely for his help and saying that if he was ever in Romania to give her a call. He had written back saying the subject had came up before, that he had considered it because he was taking his business seriously. But, he found it easy to tell her, he was concerned he'd be viewed as some kind of pimp — an e-pimp — and that this might get him into trouble with brothers and boyfriends and fathers. Alina — *you say Aleeena like this xx* — laughed that off, telling Henry he was a good employer and that not all Romanians are angry or beggars or thieves, despite what he may have heard from people who didn't know. She said she was in no way trying to con Henry, but that she was just interested in people. She said she didn't get to meet with humanity much. She said she spent her days typing the same words over and over again, and sliding the same pieces of plastic into the same holes on her body over and over again. She laughed — *hahahhahahahaha!!!* — and said that sometimes she wanted to talk to people she was not trying to get money from. She was a little bit of innocent joy amid all the adult clutter. Henry suspected she was as lonely as uniqueness.

They talked about money, among other things, in their daily emails. She told him the average wage in Romania was about $130 a month and that she was making way above average now, thanks to him. She said she worked a lot because she had pressing debts to pay each month, because her father had been in a serious, immobilising accident and his financial woes had been passed over to her. He had, she said, been a member of the secret police, the Securitate, inside the toppled regime of

Nicolae Ceausescu, the dictator who raped Romania and who was executed by a risen people on Christmas Day, 1989. Henry said he didn't know who his real father was, and Alina said hers was once known to too many people.

Soon Henry was confessing to having once watched her and others on their cams in the free chatroom area, and said that he had called himself LOP. Alina said she liked the name and hoped he had liked her. She said she didn't always dress like that. Henry said he thought she was beyond divine, but he didn't stress it any more in case he started sounding like one of her horned-up punters. He said he was sorry to say this, but that he thought she looked like she needed a good dinner. Alina had emailed a picture of herself holding a pan brimming with potatoes. *You happy mister?* she wrote. *Very*, he said, wondering how arms so thin could support a pan which was larger than her head and deeper than her body. He sent her a picture of himself clapping. She replied saying she had never seen any image of anyone who had ever viewed her webcam. She liked it, she told him. In complex pidgin which took him ten minutes to decipher, she told him he looked like a man too short to be a movie star, too narrow to be a tough guy and with too much wavy black hair to be a ruthless businessman – but that he was somehow full of possibilities all the same. She told him it was nice to know he was real. Henry felt like he was being chatted up by a babe – an unfamiliar experience – and blushed alone. It was as if, he thought as he later weighed up his day, all heaven was breaking loose.

Shuff Sheridan has been in the aircraft toilet for nineteen minutes. A queue of three has formed at the front of the plane. They're beginning to look annoyed and shake heads at each other. Henry has already sunk a little lower in case any of them know that the empty window seat beside his belongs to the brute in the toilet. By this stage the pressure has become too great, and Henry has plucked Shuff's phone from the seat pocket and switched it off. He tells himself this was the right thing to do and anyway, Shuff is his employee for the next few days. He will tell Shuff that he did it because if it had rung all the way up there in the skies, Shuff could have faced a fine of thousands. But he is just as anxious now that he has turned off as he was when it was on. He wonders if he looks as white as he feels.

The door opens with a pronounced click. A red cross disappears from the toilet sign in the cabin. Shuff emerges with a smile, winking at the woman next in line. The two men behind her smile happily at Shuff, both instantly deciding a scowl is the wrong way to greet the burly, tattooed nut whose icy eyes take in everything around him. As Shuff angles his way past, Henry watches the woman enter the tiny toilet, and he watches her come straight back out. She looks like she's seen a ghost. She looks down the plane, towards Shuff, and then to the men who had been waiting with her. She says a few dramatic words. The men are shocked and look back at Shuff, who's now almost at his seat. One of them steps past the woman and takes a look inside. Henry panics, fearing Shuff has shat all over the floor or smashed up the facilities. The man sticks his head back out and shrugs. He casts a scowl towards Shuff's back and goes in, closing and locking the door with that definite click. The red cross lights up again.

'They look shocked, mate,' ventures Henry, cool as a stir-fry, as Shuff sits back down. His cuffs are higher now, and Henry sneakily tries again to get some idea of what's written on his arms. The letters are neat, but small and bound closely together. They spiral from his wrist to God knows where. OVID.

'Who looks shocked?'

'The people waiting for the toilets.'

'Aye. I'm not fucken surprised. Big watery shite, y'know. Couple of pints came out in the one pump, easy.'

'Right.'

'Shocked me too, so it did.'

Henry can smell something that isn't shite. It wafts from Shuff as he speaks.

'You weren't smoking in there, were you?' he quizzes like a nervous teacher with an unpredictable student.

'Aye. Wee joint. You want one?'

'Bloody hell.'

'Good stuff, like. Best in Belfast.'

'I'm sure it is. You can set the alarms off in there with that.'

'I like to smoke when I shite. That alarm stuff's a myth, big lad.'

RPROV. The toilet door clicks open and the man appears, red-faced. He takes a deep breath as soon as he's out of the door. He says something to the woman who had allowed him to take her turn and she elects to let the third in line go ahead of her. The relieved man walks down the plane, stopping at Henry's row. He reaches over to Shuff with a closed fist.

'I think you forgot something,' he says.

Shuff looks up at him. 'What'd you say?'

The man shakes his fist a little, indicating that he has something in it. Shuff holds out a suspicious paw and the man drops a little package into it.

'I think that's yours. Be careful.' He walks on. Shuff looks. It's a little bag of Afghan weed, stolen from a drug dealer he met in a chip shop.

'Oh aye,' he says. He holds it up in the air, turning around in his seat. 'Thanks, big lad. Nice one.'

Henry shrinks a bit further. People whisper. How many rules can a man break on an hour-long flight? Shuff isn't counting. The words of his tattoos are proof that he's not bound by rules. He doesn't necessarily go out of his way to break them, he just doesn't take any interest in what they say.

'What time's the Budapest plane tomorrow?' he says, spreading and knocking Henry's anxious, motoring leg away.

'Half seven. It's Bucharest. Where do your mates live?' Henry's worried about Shuff's mates. He regrets agreeing to go over the night before the flight to Romania to allow Shuff to meet with whoever they are.

'Fuck knows. We're meeting in a wee bar in Knightsbridge. You know the big posh area?'

'I've heard of it. I wouldn't mind getting an early night.' At this rate, the three-hour flight the next day was going to take a heavy toll on Henry.

'Aye, dead on. I'm just saying hello to them, you know. Belfast ones, so they are. Come and meet them.'

'Yeah. I'll see. I'm not sure. They live in Knightsbridge?'

'No.'

'Oh.'

'Where you from again, Hen?'

'England. Originally. I lived in a bunch of places in the north of England.'

'What the fuck are you doing here?'

'Long story. Pin in a map, sort of thing. I just wanted to get away from things.'

'Me ears have gone half deaf, so they have. Welcome to Northern Ireland anyway, in case nobody's said it to you.'

'Thanks. And welcome to England, in ten minutes anyway.'

'Wha?'

'Welcome to England.'

'Aye.'

A man calls out from three rows behind. 'Is that big Shuff Sheridan?'

Shuff sits up and turns around. A broad smile lights up his

face. 'Snatter. Fuck's sake, what about ye?'

'Dead on mate, dead on.'

Shuff turns to Henry. 'Let us out there, big lad. I know that fucker.'

Henry sighs inside as he undoes his seat belt and lets Shuff back out into public view. The fasten-seat-belt sign comes on with a ping. He feels as if the Belfast man is like some kind of beast caged up in this steel tube for too long. He can't wait to land, to breathe fresh air, hopefully not get questioned about drug smuggling and have a sensible sit down with Shuff. He wants to draw up guidelines for the voyage ahead. It's all about keeping a low profile, he'd tell him. He hoped he would anyway, if he could summon up the guts.

> Ladies and gentlemen. As the captain has now illuminated the seat belt sign, we'd ask you to return to your seats and fasten your seat belts in preparation for landing. Thank you.

Damn it.

Henry hadn't told Shuff much about Alina, and Shuff hadn't really listened anyway. Alina and Henry had been emailing each other every day for eight weeks. Two weeks ago, she had stopped writing. She seemed to have vanished, not even appearing on camera to defile herself as she had every day since she signed up with the website. She'd told Henry about the offers to meet she'd been getting from men she performed for, and he had warned her to stay well away from them. It was a breach of the rules to meet customers in real life, and it was dangerous too. Alina knew all this, but Henry had to put himself in her position. Good money – very good money – was sometimes on offer, and anyway there are ways a girl can meet a strange man and still have someone looking out for her. She told him about St Parascheva, the Protector of her city, Protector of the entire region of Moldavia, of which Iasi – *you say Yashie like this xx* – is the capital. Henry shook his head at his screen. Alina said she visited her Saint's one-thousand-year-old bones once a month at the city's Metropolitan Cathedral, and that Parascheva kept her safe and secure. *She my strong woman!!!xx*. Henry thought she might as well pop up to Transylvania and ask Dracula to watch her back.

Ultimately, he had said that it was her choice and he wasn't going to boot her off for meeting a client in the flesh. He told her, jealously, that doing this would essentially make her a prostitute, but she said she had been working as a prostitute anyway. *My difference is I could see a face,* she wrote. Henry didn't really know what to say to that.

The last time she wrote she said that one man who had approached her about meeting had approached her again. He had explained that he was going to be in Iasi and they could at least meet for a chat. She was actively considering the idea and Henry felt she was just bouncing it off him, mind already made up, because she had nowhere else to bounce it. The man – she said he was one of her regulars – didn't seem like a bad person. Henry said yes whatever, do what you like, and left it at that. He didn't even say be careful, the last time they communicated. He hated the thought of her performing for someone in the flesh for cash, and had clenched his soft fist after pressing Send. At least he knew, he thought, that if something violent or illegal did happen, police would be able to access the user credit card accounts held by QuestorCyber, and hopefully catch the culprit. But as he didn't know what had happened, and had no proof of a crime, Romanian officialdom and embarrassing interviews about his own pornographic affairs seemed to be an unnecessary horror to get involved with.

Alina is at the front of his mind. The half-promise to himself to hook up with the best of his best girls and make sure everything was well, the promise to be a good e-businessman and immerse himself in his new life – such as it was – had all become less and less important. He had contacted QuestorCyber, telling them he wanted to review Alina's epassporte, and they had forwarded it to him. He printed it off, gathering the address she said she lived at. He rang the number, but the line was dead. He didn't know if it had ever been a real number any more than he really knew anything about her at all.

A flustered, red-faced stewardess with Daisy on her name-badge approaches Shuff eight minutes before landing.

'Sir. You have to return to your seat now.'

'In a minute, love.'

'No. Now, sir. Straight away. We're landing.'

Only a few look. Henry stares at his finger, watching it pluck away at the netting in front of him.

A camp steward called Pete enters the fray.

'Sir. We are coming into land and you are causing a danger to other passengers in the aircraft.'

Shuff smiles at him. 'Just land the fucken thing. How am I causing a danger standing here?'

Daisy tuts. 'You will be reported to police on the ground when we land. You're breaking the law, sir.'

Henry can't take any more. He unclips his seat belt. 'Shuff,' he calls, rising up and looking back. 'Come on, mate,' waving him in with a hand.

'Jesus,' says Shuff. 'These rules are a pain in the hole.'

'Will you please go back to your seat, sir?' says Daisy, squeezing her lips together in anger. This affront to her authority comes from the man who had smoked in the toilets, and she had already let that one go for the sake of an easy life. 'I don't want to have to get the police.'

'Straight away,' says Pete, pointlessly.

Shuff stands tall and reaches out, sinking Henry's heart as he takes Daisy by the hands. Pete steps forward, momentarily fired on a sprinkle of testosterone. Shuff looks down at her, into her eyes, and starts to hum. He pulls her in close.

'I won't sing it,' he whispers to her face. By now, dozens of wide eyes have turned to the scene. The plane breaks through the low clouds. Shuff starts to sing:

> Never seen you looking so gorgeous as you did tonight,
> Never seen you shine so bright, you were amazing.

He starts to sway his hips. Daisy blushes, smiles, looks at the floor and then, just a little bit, laughs. Camp Pete tilts his head to the side and breathes happily out, sharing the sudden gush of romance which has entered a part of Daisy's brain which had been dry for two years. She knew for a fact that Shuff was going to sing that bloody *Daisy Daisy* song until he said he wouldn't sing it. He'd taken her by surprise.

Shuff whispers in her ear: 'I once learned something about the word stewardess from a secretary.'

She's surprised again. Curious, a shade excited.

Quietly: 'Oh? What was that?'

Shuff smiles more, whispers closer. 'They say it's the longest word you can type with your left hand.'

Daisy cranes her neck up, her whole face grinning. She whispers back: 'What about stewardesses?'

Shuff laughs, crinkling his eyes up and becoming cuddly, hips swinging gently. He winks. Snatter starts to clap, joined instantly by his tubby wife. Others join in, and as the runway comes into clear view, the plane is booming with applause.

Shuff kisses Daisy, politely, on the lips, unhands her and

walks back to his seat. Henry allows him in, and even pats him on the back as he sits down and connects his seat belt. He knows he'd never have got away with the same act with any woman on earth.

'Crikey Shuff, you're in there, mate,' he whispers as the applause fades and the captain, suspicious of the raucous endorsement of how he flew his plane, braces for imminent touchdown.

'Anno,' says Shuff. He plucks his phone from the seat pocket, examines the blank screen and turns to Henry, disappointed. 'You need to fucken relax, big lad.'

'Yes.' Henry breathes out.

Shuff drops the phone into his shirt pocket and spreads his legs. And as the wheels connect with England, Henry's heart starts to punch him.

6

'Close that door over Rosie, for fuck's sake.'

'Hang on. I dropped me lighter.' A pause. 'Right, it's closed. Why do you always gurn at me, for fuck's sake.'

'You're always leavin it open, for fuck's sake.'

'Fuck up.'

'Give us a fucken light.'

Rosie and Della are enjoying a morning smoke in the tiny yard outside the purple back door of their east Belfast terraced home. The purple door has been attached to the same century-old house through thick and thin, and is both thick and thin itself. The frame has warped and the door has swollen, requiring a sharp tug to get it to close properly. In the centre, a badly nailed-on wooden panel hides a major fracture from one of seven raids, some by police, some by various categories of thug. Two bullet holes along its top are visible scars of a serious warning to the occupants, passed on by someone firing into the yard from the back alleyway. Carved into the door, low down, are the words *Liverpole, Rosie, Teds a big cock 4 Rosie, dellas a cunt, fuck, ur balls are fucked, fuck the Police* and *your dead*. The aged penknife which was used to carve *your dead* into the door two years ago still lies in the yard, under a car battery thoroughly chewed by a stout and deranged American pit bull called NAILER. The penknife too had been chewed, and if anyone had ever thought of picking it up, they'd have noticed that its steel blade had been misaligned by merciless jaws and teeth.

The ground has been a growing domestic rubbish tip for as long as the girls can remember. In the little space where they now stand is a gathering pile of cigarette butts, empty lighters, bits of hair, sweet wrappers, a baby's hat, beer cans, fast-food wrappers, cider cans, used condoms, bloodied rags, empty bottles, chewed old plastic and vintage magazines. Through its random, untreated ugliness are strewn enough misshapen objects to jigsaw together a jungle of stories, but no one wants to pick up any of the pieces. Few can even stand confidently among them, which is why Rosie and Della stand still, almost on their tiptoes, on the remaining four patches of now precious yard, every day. They shiver and suck hard and fast on their particular choice of lungwear. They speak loudly at each other like angry enemies meeting on a windy mountaintop.

'Who's that at the door anyway?' asks Rosie, picking the sleep out of her eyes and looking at it.

'I told ya, ya deaf bitch.' Della spits.

'I didn't hear ya, fuck's sake.'

'It's that fucken policewoman.'

'That bitch who ate my KitKat?' Rosie loves KitKats more than most things in her life.

'Aye.'

'Hungry cunt, so she is.'

'Did Mummy not tell her to leave us alone?'

'She's nat going to let them in again.'

Says Rosie: 'But she fucken talked to her about leavin us alone the last time, didn't she?'

'Yes. Didn't I fucken say yes? What fucken language do you speak?'

'THEN WHAT DID SHE FUCKEN SAY, YOU STUPID CUNT.'

'She just opened the door on the chain, so she did. She

goes, "I don't have a television", and the woman says she doesn't care.'

'Television? What the fuck's that got to do with anything?'

'Dunno. She's just freaked. They want pictures and all.'

Rosie tuts. 'Anno. Fuck's sake. She knows there's none of him.'

'Aye. She knocked again for a wee bit then, but that was all. Mummy's had enough. Fucken peelers are useless.'

'Mummy out?'

'Aye. Somewhere.'

'Where's Daddy away to anyway?'

'Fuck knows. He told mummy he needs an operation on his balls.'

'Anno. Do you think that's where he's away?'

'Nah. He's away to some foreign place to get money or somethin.'

'Right. Do you think that bitch is still standin there?'

'How the fuck would I know? What am I? Fucken X-Ray Girl?'

Della rages: 'AM JUST FUCKEN ASKIN.'

The girls – Rosie's sixteen, Della's seventeen – each light up another from their own packets. Rosie prefers Marlboro Lights and Della's into Winston. Rosie's into cider and Della prefers Bacardi Breezer. These are things they'd liked to have been able to say about themselves when, with their mother's credit card, they put their advert on an internet personals page, but the moderator had thrown out the swearing and explicit references to alcohol, drugs, sex, violence and gambling.

> Two gorgeous Belfast sisters (18) WLTM two gorgeous men for drives and long nights in France and Italy yet settera. Age, looks, unimportant. Must have good jobs and get langered. Reply Box 77298.

The reason the word *langered* got in there was because the moderator couldn't find it on his banned words list. He had already removed *like cash, hash, cigarettes, E, good drinkers, good screwers, lucky horse racing charms* and, the final line, *no gays who can't fight*.

The ad was placed eighteen months ago, but things had changed a lot since then. Both of them had found boyfriends and, in time, after a dozen responses from much older men who seemed mostly interested in threesomes, they moved on. A while later and they forgot their personals password, never even attempting to retrieve it. The concept of a *ménage à trois* revolted both of them. Not because of the dirty old men who would have been excitedly pulling at their pants, but because they'd probably have to be naked in the same room as each other. There was so much sibling tension that they knew they'd have ended up slagging each other off and fighting over the attention of their would-be lover. They don't like to share anything.

Rosie's boyfriend is Charlie, a mild-mannered spide of seventeen. He listens to music on his headphones for an average of nine hours a day and says Nice One an average of forty-one times a day. Rosie and Charlie pass time agreeably together. She talks and smokes and he nods, dances his hands on tables or knees and says Nice One.

Della's boyfriend is Muck, an eighteen-year-old spide whose eyes fill with tears when he talks of her and whose heart fills with despair when his father, a failed boxer, comes home blocked and punches him. Muck fell in love with Della after four months of standing and two months of dating. He works in a jeweller's and gets discount on discount gold, lavishing it on his girlfriend again and again. She shines in the sun. Della is in love with Muck and is close to running away with him in the increasingly certain knowledge that they have a dream to live out in another part of the world.

'That fucken sun over the wall is blindin me.' Della puts a hand up over her eyes, like a misplaced salute.

'You're fucken glowin.'

'Fuck off.'

'I've me back to it so I don't give a fuck.' Rosie salutes Della, taking the piss.

Della looks down at her feet on the two low islands amid all the higher crap. 'I can't turn away from it on these wee spots. I'd have me nose against the fucken door.'

'Tough shite.'

'Fuck up.'

They stand their ground in silence, drawing away on the cigarettes like it's a race.

Della pipes up after considering what she'll do today, knowing that a visit to school isn't looking likely.

'You going standin tonight?' she asks.

'Dunno. Muck's ringin me later. You not seein Charlie?'

'Aye. He's comin round after he goes up the town. He's got some CDs to get off someone or somethin.'

'Muck's buyin a car, so he is.'

'Is he fuck.'

'Aye. He is. We'll bring it over anyway for youse all to see.'

'Youse going to drink in it or what?'

'Dunno. Might get out and drink with youse all for a bit first.'

'Is Muck C. Hammer gonna take you away in it?'

'Shut up. Don't call him that.'

Rosie laughs. 'He wants to get the boat and get away to fuck. He toal me.'

'Shut up. You know nathin about it.'

'What are youse going to run away with? That fucken jeweller's pays him nathin.'

'Shut up, you bitch. Muck's goin to sort it out.'

'Aye, right. You'll be standin here with me in ten years time.'

'I fucken won't, you know. We'll be away to fuck. What would I want to stay here for?'

'Robert.' Rosie likes to play with the word. She shouldn't. It's loaded.

'Aye, right. Like they're goin to find him? Me arse. Fucken gypsies are always gettin away with that. They've no hearts.'

'Aye.'

'Fuck's sake.'

'You gonna send me a postcard?'

'Shut up, you cheeky bitch. I'm goin in.'

'Aye, me too. I hope that fucker's gone. I'm not talkin to no more fucken nosy peelers.'

'Me neither. Eat you out of house and home, so they would.'

Frank the Fess feels the vibration in his steel prison as the door slams violently below him. He had woken to an exchange of words, but he's not sure what was said. He isn't sure either how long he's slept for, but suspects he's had a few hours on and off during the long, cold dark. His hands are now dry and hard and he can't feel much of his body. He tries to stretch his limbs, aching to hear a crack of bone, but very little moves. He feels like he's turning into some kind of sponge, soaking up whatever it is he lies in. He considers that this situation may be his last. He wonders now what will become of that small pot of wealth he had just recently left to no one.

Some weeks earlier, nippy Rhonda at the nursing home had tried to get her fat little hands on some of Frank's fat little wealth. She had tried to bribe some out of him, but he had spotted it straight away. She'd taken an interest in the manner of his arrival at the home, circling him and smiling for a few days before moving in for the kill. She had known that, save for two ambulance staff, frail Frank had arrived alone. No one had been there to help him settle in, and no one had spoken up for him when he tried to protest, in confused whispers, against his incarceration. Social Services had been clear about his case, that he was no longer fit to live alone, that he was losing his mind, that this dying place was the only home in which he could live. Frank had known this policy to be wrong but his forced, legal removal from his home was but a tiny event lost on everyone except Frank himself, and his new acquaintance, Rhonda.

She had asked him, three days into his unhappy stay, about his family, his friends, about the people who would surely reflect guiltily on this sudden upset to his old life. Perhaps foolishly, he had gathered his jumbled thoughts and eventually told her the truth. He said there was no one, that there was nothing, that all had died or moved or ceased to care. But Rhonda suspected that Frank was not telling her everything, and had begun cuddling up to him, a vulture hovering over his place of death. He had little choice but to have her around him, but he was still in control of the fate of his few earthly possessions.

'You are hoping I will offer you some money,' he had whispered during a moment of clarity as she caressed his old thigh.

'Don't be silly,' she said, her hand wandering closer to his crotch.

'You are supposed to take care of me,' he said. 'I'm not supposed to bribe you for my comfort.'

'You're talking nonsense again,' she replied, her bountiful breasts moving closer to his face. 'You always talk nonsense, Frank.'

'I'm not, Rita,' he managed, as images of that full bosom bounced nakedly through the clutter of his mind.

'My name is fucking Rhonda,' she said. And she whispered: 'Don't piss me off, you dozy old man.'

After a difficult appointment, Frank had instructed his solicitor to sell his home, and ordered his wealth be secured elsewhere, to ensure that no one could ever claim a cut of it. His solicitor told him the house was already under offer, and that a percentage of its value would go towards paying for his care in the nursing home.

After the sale, Frank, feeling the end of his days approaching, had a think and arranged his final visit to the solicitor. Together they drew up a plan for the disposal of what remained. He hadn't mentioned Rhonda at all.

Frank told her this later that day, explaining that the money's fate was sealed, that she might as well forget about it, that he couldn't tip her even if he wanted to. That was when those fat hands began to jab and bite at his legs like rats, and Frank had grown ever quieter.

'Many old men are more sensible and generous than you,' she had whispered to him, pushing one of his fingers back further than it was designed to go.

'And most people are kinder than you,' he had mumbled, working hard to extract the words from his tired mind.

'You can't fucking take it with you,' she had whispered, letting his finger fall back into place.

'No. And neither can you,' he had returned.

He shakes her from his head, hoping her memory will vanish forever. He wants to try not to reflect, but to think forward. And as he does, an idea begins to brighten him. It's a thought about those voices, the voices below. For they have surely confirmed that he's no longer in or around the confines of that nursing home. The voices are too alive, too burdened with the stuff of the living, not the dying. It's good to know he's learning something from his immediate environment. It had initially seemed so dead.

He moves his hands down to his naked crotch and places his shrivelled penis in such a position that he can pee over himself. There isn't much of it – he hasn't consumed anything since his kidnapping – but it's enough to clean part of one sore hand, to free it of some of the stinking, gooey, dehydrating mud. As he closes his fingers on the now cleaner hand, he feels that it's still greasy. This mud, he thinks, is definitely not mud. His head aches like it's being squeezed in a vice.

Frank the Fess is losing what he heard the girls talking about. He tries to remind himself. There was something about leaving, about getting the boat. The girls have Belfast accents, he thinks, and they're talking about one of them getting a boat with her boyfriend in his new car. Most likely this is a boat to Britain. He smiles now at his detections, at his work on the little puzzle he has been presented with. The girls spoke as if they were directly underneath where he lies. That places him at least slightly higher than the average height of a young woman. Say five feet five. He's going to assume he's about seven feet in the air. The girl who wants to run away is important too, he considers. Her words tell him he's in some kind of space where people can speak freely about their plans, and suggests that they aren't aware of his presence above. Whoever put him in here isn't here now. But, of course, that could change at any time.

His attempts at movement have allowed some feeling to flow back into his legs. It's good to know that the blood in his veins still has direction, that it isn't coagulating like the mess in which he lies. Lifting them up or even just bending them at the knee would be a further joy, he thinks. His head is glued and his trunk and bottom are numb beyond feeling. But there is hope for the legs, and after three minutes he begins to draw his feet back. His knees are finally bending and it feels so good. He reaches his cleanest hand to his right thigh, to try to give it some kind of weak massage.

He feels something stuck to it and slowly tries to grip whatever it is and bring it to his face. In the dim light, he can see that underneath a coat of grime is a light-coloured article. It's lightweight yet strong and springy, as if it would bounce if dropped from a height. He feels around it again. He wipes it more. He knows this texture. He knows the form of this new piece of evidence, the way it's shaped, the way it reacts to pressure. He knows it has design, that it's more than some kind of random piece of rubbish. He feels, when he presses it, that it has neat little indentations, perhaps marks where it had been attached to something else. He rubs his thumb over them and decides that these are not part of it, that they interrupt the pure, fine curves of the object. He thinks, if this is something that has been designed, then it must be manmade. But what purpose could it have? He thinks further. Then it comes to him. The size of it, the quantity of the softer material.

It's a bone, a young bone – young because of the developing pattern of cartilage protecting it, ready to form into hard bone as it sprouts. The shape of it, the size of it, the age and innocence of it. He runs it tenderly around in his hand. It's a baby's leg bone, a tiny, damaged tibia, probably taken from a host not more than a few weeks old. Somehow or other a baby had given up a leg. Perhaps it was in this steel place that the infant died.

Frank puts it gently back into the unknown mud in which he lies, re-covering it, burying it. He fills his lungs with a sigh. He wonders how Hell will compare with this.

My dear old friend,

I appeared in a newspaper. It was leaked that I had confessed to an alarming number of crimes, and a journalist arrived at my house. I confessed all to him too. I told him about all the crimes I had committed, including the murder. He took it all down and another man took my picture. It appeared the following day. They called me Frank the Fess. The university called me in and said they had to let me go. I don't mind. In a way, everything that is going on now is a great relief. I am being regarded as a fool.

Detective Sergeant Ryan is not a happy man. He came round to my house two days ago to say so. He explained that it was normal policy to ignore serial confessors, but that I had overstepped a mark and was wasting police time. I now know the mark to be somewhere around twenty-two letters, seventeen phone calls and five visits to the station. He's a decent man. He reminded me of one of my old students, one of the good ones. I told him this and he sighed and sat down. He asked for a cup of tea, which I duly made, and he asked me to take him through things while he ate a bun I had found. I can't remember where I found it. He wanted to know why I had thrown away my oh-so respectable once-a-month lecturing post at the university. The explanation was so simple. I told him that he had not been listening. I said I had become a criminal and the university had no choice but to dissociate itself from me. He left soon after that. He said the tea was good but he did not finish the bun.

I must also tell you that the Fan called again today. He still talks to me like I'm a priest. He keeps no secrets. I

told him what I'd been doing and he laughed. He told
me he had punched a traffic warden. I hope it wasn't
caught on camera because I'm going to write to
Detective Sergeant Ryan and claim it. Do you think
I am fit to break someone's nose? Nor I. I might say
I had some kind of knuckle buster. Is it buster or
duster? I don't know.

My Jack Russell left for a long time during the
week. He stayed out overnight but came back the next
day. That's a first. He's been acting strangely for a few
days now. He watched me set light to the living room
curtains with great interest. I need to learn more about
destruction, I told him, if I'm going to be such a prolific
criminal. I told him I had to have some idea of what
I'm talking about. This all scared him a little, I think.
I was able to extinguish the fire minutes later, but he
seems to have been shocked. This act may have made
him leave for the night. I hope he knows what he's
doing.

Regards, old friend,

Francis Cleary

7

Three weeks ago in a flat ten floors above Iasi, Alina was preparing for work. She drank the daily glass of warm, thin, tangy orange juice into her thin body and watched what she could of the sunrise. She rinsed the glass and put it beside her plate in the kitchen area, a place stripped to its bare essentials and sold off. Another day, thought Alina, her sleeping space turned to workspace, another $1.99 on occasional minutes, split 60/40 in my favour.

In the morning in Alina's flat it was like those bygone days when folk rose early to make the most of the light. Her circumstances insisted on this step back in time, so she never missed a single sunrise. A sunrise is a splendid-looking thing anyway, although from where Alina lived, it wasn't much more than shades of polluted light falling in from above the dead, grey, equal, awful tower on the other side of the street.

She straightened up her bed and propped her pillow against the wall on which she would lean for much of the day. She scooped up the green teddy bear from the floor and set it in the centre of her bed, apologising into its ear as she went. She reached down again, picked up her dildo and laid it, in view, beside the stuffed toy which she wouldn't christen with a name. She threw her bottle of cheap baby oil onto the bed, dropped her old boxer shorts and slipped into her yellow cotton knickers. She wouldn't wear a top of any kind today – it was something new to try. She went into the bathroom, scrubbed her teeth with an empty brush and ran three handfuls of cold water over her short, bright face and through her Bovril hair. She went to her computer, powered it up and checked that the camera would catch all of her image. She got back onto the bed, put on some lipstick and leaned against the wall, legs wide like a whore.

The computer was a mess. It struggled every day with the biblical plague of viruses which had infected it, and it crashed more times than she could be bothered to count. She didn't know how to get shot of the viruses, short of paying someone to do it for her. She'd conducted some research online, but protection is the first line of defence for computers, and her protection had already failed. Some kind of semi-obsolete firewall and anti-virus software had already been installed on the machine when she bought it through a newspaper ad, but it was largely useless. She'd suspected some uselessness when it was delivered to her door in a damp cardboard box by a man in a hurry. The man showed her what to plug into what, how to work the webcam and how to sign up with a cheap, local service provider he knew whom she could pay with a monthly cheque. He obviously had a fair idea of what she was planning to do. He said the webcam had a long lead, and that Alina would be able to place it anywhere it might be required. He would have had a twinkle in his eye as he explained these things to her, only he had met more girls like Alina than he could be bothered to count.

Alina's research taught her how much efficient PC protection would cost. So, with The Policy calling the tune, she'd take that step only if absolutely necessary. As it was, most of the time it was all systems go, so help didn't seem necessary. Occasionally the thing crashed when a customer had logged on to private chat and started paying, but up to now most of them had come excitedly back to her minutes later when she managed to get back online. Only when it was seriously interfering with her performances and losing her money would she consider treating it to an overhaul.

When she'd first tried to work the computer, she'd been baffled. She'd listened to the man's instructions but didn't want to say that she didn't know what he or they meant. After a long day's work alone, she had managed to get all the wires in the right places and go online. But it became ever more daunting when she began to get some understanding of how vast, fast and intimidating this international network is, and frightening to think that she was going to have to muscle in and claim her own space in a world that, she was tempted to believe, didn't actually exist. It was baffling when she explored, trying to use the thing to research itself, keying in questions in broken English and receiving answers which just led her further down brightly lit paths which led from and to places she had no idea about. The whole thing was as confusing as a broken shower, running hot and cold and tipping this way and that, failing her when she tried to take control.

All her searching was going to have to be in English if it was going to reach deep into the internet, she knew. Her language's presence on the web was ignored by the world she needed to communicate with, so she would have to ignore it too. But her English wasn't bad. It was as good as it is with most young Iasians these days, although maybe a little worse. But the frustration of not knowing technical words or how to search for what she was going to do with something without knowing what it was called, led to angry exchanges between her and the search engines. She knew swear words in English, thanks to television and rare tourists who liked to drink cheaply and talk to the local girls, and knew that they meant something more significant than everyday non–swear words. What if they made the computer pay more attention? It had been a curious brainwave. She ended up banging on the keys, bashing questions into Google and Yahoo, hoping they would feel her temper and just answer her call.

> How in bloody name hell do I find good internet pictures work?????!

This led her directly to scenes of violence, to pictures of damaged noses and images of the devil, of cinemas and of a man digging a road. Her small temper flared.

> How in name of fuck do I see internet pictures work?

This cued up some pornography, and it wasn't a bad development. She was able to pause on the pages and soak up an understanding of what it was that people liked to see. She advanced.

> What is the pictures that move for sale??

Films, movies, house movers and piles and piles of useless pages filled with web words about acting, yoga and buying property. She sighed.

> What is the fucking pictures that move for sale???

Again, back to the porn. Sexual intercourse and short and surprising little movies of various sex acts. And then she saw the new English word she had been looking for, and chalked herself up a victory: webcam. From there she began looking up live webcam sites and began to learn the craft absorbed and perfected by so many girls like her in so many countries like Romania.

At first she poked around in the free chatrooms under the name of BILL, noticing what the men said to the girls in the little windows, and what the cool and confident girls said in response. When she felt she had a handle on what was driving them, she started to log in as KYLIE and noticed that, immediately, some men turned towards her. There were no pictures for them to look at, and not yet a live image, just five letters in a box in a place where men talked openly, anonymously, about sex. KYLIE could have been anybody, any kind of person from anywhere in the world, but they turned to the letters of her name and asked again and again if she liked to look at sexy girls and large erections. When she said no, they slammed her for being in there and for watching the men's personal chatter. When she said yes, most of them turned to her and demanded to know things that she felt would only ever be the business of her future husband. When she looked deeper into it all, and learned more from the girls than from the men, she logged in under the name NADIA. It made all the men in the room turn to her, and caused many of them to ask her personal things that not even she knew the answers to. There's definitely something in the names, she thought. The men love the Eastern European girls, she thought. It's because we look nice, but we're poor, she thought. They never once asked her if she was a guy. They stepped into fantasy land when they logged on, and they didn't want the facts to get in the way.

In time, after plucking up the courage to take her nude virginity onto the internet, she turned eighteen and signed up with Woundlicker Dot Com, simply by clicking a Models Wanted button on the site and filling out a form which, with the aid of a mailed document, rigorously proved she was not underage. After a hundred deep breaths and a hundred false starts, she began making good and legal money, clocking up the minutes and withdrawing the cash from her simple epassporte account with a plastic card.

She played around with her name, and she made more money. She learned that when she called herself a Bitch or a Mistress or a Horny Housewife, they came running. She learned that her breasts were too small for many men and that close-ups of her small, squarish feet made others want to die for her or marry her. There were those, she found, who liked her to talk as if she was going to hit them, ridicule them or make them dress as girls. But there was always an element, a growing group of often pleasant men who told her that her youth was her beauty, that her big chestnut eyes and symmetrical dimples were her fortune, that her flat, thin, pubescent frame was her fame, and that she was no dominatrix. As time passed, they told her over and over again that she was too cute, too sweet and too little, and that it was just right for them. When she called herself LITTLEMISS, or the even sillier LILBIT, she made more money. When she became more innocent and behaved like a youngster, like a child with a childish name, she hit her earning stride. There's so much attached to the name, she told herself. I am not a saucy secretary or a woman who can convince men that I am the one they'll learn from, she thought. I'm just a girl whom men want to love and spoil and protect at first, and then ruin. And it was no problem. The Policy had no opinions. Alina had nothing to lose. Be little, she told herself, and earn big.

One day the regular customers who liked Little Alina noted how she had raised, by one dollar, her price per minute, in line with her confidence. They revolted, dashing her name in the chatroom, saying she had no respect for her clients, causing a mutiny among the men who had told her they wanted to give her everything they owned. She was embarrassed. She tried to tell them that she appreciated their time and would never want them to think she was trying to fleece them. They called her a TEASE and a WHORE and a ROMANIAN GYPSY BITCH and ignored her. Alina had no pride to swallow. She dropped her price back to $1.99 per minute with a delicate shrug, a little sorry that she had hurt the feelings of others.

She announced it on her belly with lipstick. Things returned to normal, and she became busy once again. She continued where she had left off, pretending she was being loved and used by strangers for the rest of her time online. She was typecast, a cheap Lolita, and it was fine. She would work with it. She had to.

Her regulars liked it when she logged on one day against a new backdrop. She had taken a large piece of yellow and blue wallpaper from an orphanage bin and pinned it on her wall so that it formed the background to the full camera shot. It featured happy little teddies and rabbits. The men told her to put her hair up in bunches, to suck her thumb and to tell them she loved them. They liked it when she kept her vagina shaved and pushed a thick black sex toy into her rectum. They liked it when she played like a little girl, showed them they had her trust, called them mister, and smoked cigarettes and coughed. In a way, she figured the best research she had ever conducted was in her own head, recalling herself as a younger girl and adding into her behaviour a disturbingly unreal fantasy reaction to an abuse which she had never suffered.

It was word of mouth that had led to Alina's dramatic career change from trainee saleswoman to webcam starlet. A girl she had worked with in her last job had quit shortly before her, instructing a store manager to stick his lamps where they wouldn't shine. Alina had been shocked by her outburst, but curious at her news. She had explained, hushed and cool, to Alina earlier that day how she had bought a computer and started working from home, and that the rewards were good. At that stage in Alina's life, electrical illuminations held more promise – the company had a large outlet in Iasi, and a larger one in Bucharest. But, in what Alina saw as fate, the girl's words would soon prove to have been worth hearing.

The computer had cost her, but it was a necessary expense

if she was going to make any headway. Her father, beaten into a coma, was being taken care of by the state in a private hospital in Bucharest. The government had stepped in, acknowledging that he had given his services to the long-gone Ceausescu regime as a servant of his country, not as a man who wanted to bully his people. Tens of thousands of people in Iasi had worked in one way or another for the regime, with whole families tasked to secretly watch for troublemakers of any kind or kin. The Securitate had been ruthless, but it operated with a robust efficiency that interested and impressed many Western democracies long before its fall. It constantly targeted conspirators and frequently hit more than its targets, but it was the way society had been stitched together in those days. Some say, with an eye on shadowy figures who still hold a lot of power in the nation today, that it's sometimes as if it still is.

Alina's Dad, a small, strong man called Gogu, had been a middle-ranking Securitate officer, an effective operator with an instinctive nose and a learned paranoia that he would never shake. When the new era came, he wasn't hated because of his past. Those sins were in the past and they stained too many people. Life would have been insufferable if you were the sort of person who fully hated one in three of the people in your town. But it was when Gogu was in the wrong bar at the wrong time and said the wrong thing that he got a beating more severe than even he had ever witnessed. The man who laid the final blow said that Gogu deserved it for destroying his family and fucking his country.

A grisly, bad-breathed official called on Alina after her Dad had been taken to Bucharest. He told her she was now responsible for her father's debts, and she was lucky that the state would cover the cost of looking after him. People looked at her from the doorways of the big grey block as the man explained loudly how much she owed and how long she had to pay it. The debt was large, the time was short, and he wanted the maximum she could give him each month. She took his papers and signed them with a tiny, unhappy squiggle, then slipped back into the tiny flat they had moved to after Gogu was laid off and her mother had died from an accelerated cancer.

Immediately she launched her plan to beat the debts, quit the lamps, make money from home and leave Romania. She would do it with the help of The Policy. She wanted it to be her new religion, and treated it with the respect she felt it deserved. She thought of it as an instruction from her father, and wished only that he had told her of his debts – he'd been laid off with nothing and a shark had swum in to help him raise his daughter – before the beating which took him away. But he rarely spoke with Alina about the bad things in life, only the good. He had always tried to be a better man, but sometimes he got it wrong. His whole career had been testimony to that. In turn, Alina too decided that, in her monthly prayers to him, she would never reveal what she was doing to make her evermore lonely life progress. She only ever told him things that were good.

Alina pig-tailed her hair with a couple of bands, put the keyboard across her lap, and topless LILBIT in the yellow cotton knickers went live. Business was slow on Tuesday mornings, with most of the Americans having faced up to a week of work ahead. The Europeans too slowed down at this stage of the cycle, but there were always a few people around, their half-cut minds turned to cutting-edge masturbation, ready to pay for more than just a couple of minutes worth of teasing. One of these men was online. He was new. His name was THELAT. He told LILBIT how pretty she was before logging into private and telling her he couldn't stand watching all those men lusting over her and not paying her a thing. He told her he had her to himself now and just wanted to talk. They chatted about things, about how he liked living in Glasgow and that the girls he knew weren't as gorgeous as the girls in Eastern Europe.

On his instruction, she brought her knickers down to her knees, lay back and lifted her legs, open as a door. There was silence from his keyboard. Alina tried to reach for hers, without losing balance, to press a few buttons and check that all was well. As gracefully as possible, she retrieved it and managed to write *this ok baby? xx* with one finger, but no response arrived. She stayed put for another four minutes before twisting her neck and checking her screen to see if he was still there. And yes, he was still online, still accepting her feed from the other end of Europe, still paying his way. She bounced up and down a bit, showing how flexible she was in that easy, fat-free S-bend. She parted her buttocks and her vagina, and rubbed both before licking her hand in overacted ecstasy. Still nothing. A minute later, she dropped her legs back down and sat forward on her bed, smiling at the man. They're usually quiet when they play with themselves, she thought, but this man's really quiet. She sat, looking into the camera, face on her hand, occasionally writing *what I do baby? xx,* occasionally licking her lips, hugging her breasts and turning around and opening her body, running out of ideas without any orders. The Policy would not allow her to turn the camera off or kick the customer out, as was her right, so she just kept on improvising.

After another seventeen minutes of toying with herself, after stretching some more of the virginity she still technically possessed, she sat forward with her head in both hands. She stared into the lens, wondering who was at the other end of the wire, and she started to make faces at it. Eleven minutes later, and it disconnected. Not a word was said. Did a wife arrive home and find a husband asleep in front of Alina, his penis shrivelled and coated with drying semen? Did he die from a heart attack and fall from his seat, crashing the computer to the ground as he went? Had she killed him? Did he just run out of credits? Who knows? Alina wondered about these things, and sometimes she worried, but these concerns soon left her mind. It wasn't as if she'd met someone. She'd had an unbroken half hour of work and that was the kind of thing that really mattered to her these days. She got herself a piece of bread and a cigarette and LILBIT went back to work.

HARDEST	coochie coooooo!!!
FREEWALES	hi sweety:−)
NORM	hi!!! Luving u baby!!!
NSWROGER	show cunt and I PRIVATE with u
HARDEST	show pussy baby
NORM	nice tits
NSWROGER	I SAID I PRIVATE IF U SHOW NOW
FREEWALES	agreed norm
LILBIT	pussy in pvt honey only xx
NORM	yep. A real cutie
FREEWALES	where from lilbit?
NSWROGER	FUCKING BITCH. DIRTY FUCKING BITMN
HARDEST	Cut it out roger
NSWROGER	FUCK YOU GAY MAN
FREEWALES	im from wales, u no it?
NORM	yeah roger, no need for it
GANDALF	hi baby!!!! U 2 cute!!!!
LILBIT	hi gand. Wales at England free?

NSWROGER	NORMS A QUEER AIDS BASTARD
FREEWALES	nooooooooooooo! Not England!!! Close but deffo not England!!!!!!!
NORM	rogers sniffs his grandma panties
LILBIT	who want pvt with me?? Who want kiss me???xxxxxxx
GANDALF	u show me some puss lil thing?
FREEWALES	we're not English we're welsh!!! Best country in da worldddddddd!!!!
NSWROGER	shes a bitch Gandalf
HARDEST	bitch has got me hard. Looks like a lolitttttaaaa!!!!!
LILBIT	see pussy in pvt baby xxx come on xx
GADAKA	Hello Alina.
GANDALF	who asked for ur fucking opinion??
LILBIT	hi gadaka baby!!!
NSWROGER	GANDALFS A BIG GAY WIZARD
GADAKA	Let me take you away from all this.
LILBIT	welcome in private!!!!!!
GADAKA	Hi Alina. Have you been good?
LILBIT	always good!!! Xxx
GADAKA	I imagine so.
LILBIT	how u feel baby??
GADAKA	Very good, thank you. And you?
LILBIT	Ive had good day. 1 looooong man from glassgo
GADAKA	I don't want to know. I told you. I hate them.
LILBIT	okay honey sorry I 4get xxx
GADAKA	Did you do what I said?
LILBIT	yes of course!
GADAKA	Well? What did you buy?

LILBIT	the speciel skirts an cloths!!! Xx
GADAKA	Good girl.
LILBIT	u keep ur promise 2 me??
GADAKA	Yes, of course.
LILBIT	when baby???
GADAKA	See you on Friday. Clear your diary.
LILBIT	mmmmmmm baby. Cant wait 2 cu. Sooooo much luv 4u aby
GADAKA	Snap.

8

The idiotic old woman won't shut up about Earl Grey tea. She's been talking about tea since Shuff and Henry got onto the Tube, and the Earl Grey variety is her one-sided conversation of choice. She's got very little to say about it, yet she's said it once and repeated it twice already.

'I do find it too perfumed,' she whines again from the seat in front of Henry and Shuff, nose rising higher and flaring. She's got one of those accents that isn't as posh as she'd like it to be. She's moved to the Shires and probably knows someone who knows the Queen.

Henry is as embarrassed as he is annoyed. This is his native island now. He knew he was going to feel a measure of responsibility for absolutely everything crap or weird or awkward that happened in England. It's a heavy cross to bear.

'It's certainly delicate, but I find it too perfumed. Yes, light. But too perfumed.'

Shuff's eyes have scanned the train and settled on a guy at the end of the carriage who, in under a minute, will start bellowing a ferocious Matabele warrior chant. Shuff doesn't give a fuck about the Earl Grey woman. His dirtying white shirt cuffs are down to the wrist, almost fully covering his tattoos. IDE. Earl Grey is just some man with a big house.

The white African straightens, then morphs into a pose of showpiece intimidation.

'O salanini zinini, o salanini zinini, o salanini zinini ze'skote zaKaya.' He's grabbing deep into his chest, staring around with sharp twists to his neck, looking at no one. 'Ze'skote zaKaya.'

Shuff cocks his head with the honesty of a dog, intensely interested in the dramatic, deep sounds of an origin about which he knows nothing. There are times when he just marvels at the world, at people from beyond what he knows so very well.

'I just find the flavour is too perfumed,' the old woman says. 'It's not my favourite. No, definitely not.'

The train drums its way through a station with a blur for a name, pounding a million pints of blood through an artery and towards the heart of the big city. Henry's feeling hotter. It must be because he's underground. Please, he thinks, let that be the reason.

'Fuck me,' says Shuff, cutting loudly over the African, legs at right angles on the edge of the seat. 'It reminds me of prison in here, Hen. Place is mental.'

Henry nods, not able to handle that sentence, or anything much of what is going on around him. He thinks of his foster mother at the other end of the country, but pushes the thought aside.

Shuff turns again and whispers: 'I loved prison. It's easy as fuck.'

Henry says nothing.

'That's where I met yer man Snatter, the cunt on the plane. He did a couple of months for cars. He's a good lad.'

Before he could stop himself, and just as Earl Grey started again, Henry was asking it: 'What were you in for?'

He wanted to know, but he didn't know if he wanted to know so badly that it was worth offending Shuff over it.

'I went out of court through the wrong door.'

'Oh, right.'

Was that a real answer? Maybe that's what ex-prisoners say,

their shield of mystery, a polite piss-off and-mind-your-own-business.

She goes: 'I tried it just the once, but I found it too perfumed.'

The African ends his display and starts walking through the train, shaking a blue woolly hat and smiling like it's all gone well. It has. Henry reaches into his pocket, unable to avoid giving to charity when it can see him. Shuff leans forward, blocking his path.

He says: 'Who the fuck are you talking to, Missus?' The African walks on and away, hat beginning to jingle.

The woman turns, eyes wide and wild with the interruption. 'My husband, if you don't mind,' she scratches, breathing out hard at the end.

Shuff shakes his head. 'Listen love, you're sitting on yer own, fuck's sake.'

'My husband hears everything.'

'Then say something else, for fuck's sake. Tell him something dirty. That's what he'll want to hear. Perfume's bollocks.'

Henry pipes up. He wants to pull Shuff away from the woman. She's well into her seventies and in some form of grief. This is rude. Has Shuff no bloody manners at all? 'She's talking about tea, Shuff. Earl Grey's a tea.'

'She's talking about perfume, Henry. You should listen more.'

Shuff turns to the woman again, her lips sealed tight. She looks at him and then looks away.

Says Shuff, after his idea has crystallised: 'Remind him about the smell of sex, ye girl ye. That's perfume.' Shuff gently laughs at his own words.

The woman turns to him, lips pursed. Shuff laughs again, a louder, shorter, deeper chuckle. His chubby cheeks flatten when he expels the sound.

'He wouldn't have that conversation,' she says.

Henry disowns the situation and thinks of sending his foster mother a letter of some kind.

Shuff whispers: 'It's your conversation, love. Get randy with him.' It's a suggestion that will, later that day, give her something radical to think about.

Rattling through the dark, Henry spots an arch in a wall that, if he bricked it up from the inside, he could sit in for ages and ages and no one would know.

Says Shuff, some time later, alighting from a taxi after they'd checked into a hotel (Shuff had brought only a suspiciously small bag): 'Sure, I used to think the Queen ran the tourist industry.'

'What?' Henry laughs, tipping the driver and smiling, feeling better about being in England and being with Shuff. They'd shared a joke and a laugh after the woman left the train with a miniscule nod to the Belfast man. They'd laughed at the prospect of her heading home to talk dirty to herself. It's as if ice has now been broken between the two men. Henry can at least talk a little, and he does appreciate feeling somehow protected from the worrying eccentricities of London. He feels that Shuff would step up to a challenge, to a knife-wielding maniac, if one came along. He feels that if he lost his mind, Shuff might just wait with him.

Says Shuff: 'Aye. I mind someone telling me something about the Queen being behind the tourist industry, or being a big part of it or something. I just thought she must work for it. Run it, you know?'

'Oh, right. No, she doesn't do much work.'

'I know that now, ya gonk. I was about fucken twelve or something. I'm just saying.'

Shuff closes the taxi door and they walk along Sloane Street, Knightsbridge. They can sense the wealth. Henry has a packet of pills in a pocket. There are a few more in his luggage at the hotel, just in case.

He says: 'I used to think breasts were a con. You know, I wasn't sure if women really had them or not.' Henry looks down at the street and blushes. Hopefully Shuff misheard him and thinks he said anything else.

Shuff straightens his lips and nods, treating the words of idiocy with a surprisingly healthy drop of respect. 'Aye, they're weird as fuck when you're a wee lad,' he says. 'You have to rule out the possibilities.'

Henry's pleased with that. He'd never told anyone about it before, and would never have expected a reaction which didn't involve the word Wanker. Maybe they'd even get on well. He raises no objections as Shuff turns a hard left into a side street. There's a pub.

'We'll just get a wee one in here first, big lad. The boys are in some other bar round here somewhere.'

'No problem.'

In the bar, at the bar, Shuff lifts the only free stool, sits on it and spreads. 'Sorry, big lad,' he says, eyes scrunching. 'Me fucken balls are killing me.'

'No problem.' Henry has a cold flush.

They each get a pint of bitter from a pump. Henry pushes his lightweight hair back, and his ever-so-slightly mismatched eyes scan the peculiar names on the beer taps, reminding him of old England. Shuff drinks deeply, giving himself a white moustache, and breathes out with the satisfaction of a bad actor in a soap opera. Henry wants to do the same thing, but doesn't in case it looks like he's copying. The barman is from County Fermanagh. He's tall and broad and kind and wears a new-looking, chunky gold Claddagh ring on his wedding finger.

'I miss Fermanagh,' says the barman to Shuff as he pours the second round, clinking the glass on both the fizzing nozzle and that gold ring. 'I used to be a big man for the football.' He sets Shuff up with a single vodka as a chaser.

Shuff nods. 'Aye, Gaelic football?'

'Aye.'

'Never played it.'

'It's a good game. Fast, you know?'

'Aye. They're all good games if you're any fucken good at them.'

'You're right there, boy.'

The barman leaves to serve his next customer, a Kiwi.

Henry turns to his Protector. He feels that he at least looks like he's a bit of a lad, sitting here with this impossibly confident hard man. RANDD. Henry's gathered that the barman is most likely a Catholic, that Shuff is most likely Protestant. It's a little bit of Northern Ireland conditioning. He's pleased with himself.

He says: 'I was told once that warm weather was when God tilted his sword to the sun. You know, that he'd shine it on you?'

Shuff glances at Henry. It's not a positive look. Henry blushes. He thinks that's the stupidest thing he's ever said.

'I'd get a mirror if that was the case,' says Shuff. 'Shine it back at the cunt.'

Henry looks at the bar taps again. Has he gone too far? Maybe Shuff doesn't like to entertain the same odd kind of thoughts that Henry does after all. He doesn't remember hearing anyone call God a cunt before.

Shuff downs the vodka and begins his next beer. Big mouthfuls. He could probably store it in those fat but firm cheeks like a hamster. He turns back to Henry.

'What age are you?'

'Twenty-six.'

'Right. Yohan said you were adopted or something?'

'Yes.'

'Has your name changed then?'

'Yes.'

'And?'

'What?'

'Tell me about it.'

'Okay, well, my surname changed a couple of times. It's easier that way.'

'What were they?'

'Well, Chancellor was the first name I had. I'm Sender now.'

'Chancellor.' Shuff laughs. 'Fuck's sake. Lend us a quid.'

Henry's embarrassed again. How bloody English can you get? 'I was Delaware and then Harrison for a while too.'

'Delaware. Fuck's sake.'

'That was when I lived near Manchester.'

'Where else did you live?'

'A village in Lancashire, then for a while in Derby, then Newcastle.' A pause. 'Upon Tyne.'

'Right.'

'I knew a guy in Newcastle who ended up in jail. He could get people fake birth certificates and licences and stuff. Not that I'm talking about jail or anything.' Oh God.

'Right.' Shuff looks bored.

'He still does it, now that he's out. I could probably get some if you ever wanted one.'

Shuff drinks again. 'Right. What the fuck would I want with a birth certificate?'

Shit. 'I don't mean anything. I was just thinking maybe there would be something you could do with one of them.'

'Me? I could do with one of them?'

'No. I mean, anyone. You can do all sorts of things with identity stuff these days, can't you?'

'Me?'

'No. People. Not you.'

'Birth certs aren't hard to get, big lad. They're not exactly hens' teeth or anything.'

'I suppose.'

'Not that anyone wants fucken hens' teeth.'

'True. I wouldn't know a hen's tooth if it bit me.' Henry thinks how they don't have teeth. Shuff can't recall what a hen looks like. He thinks of a turkey, but lets the thought drop.

Says Shuff: 'Do you want to change your name again, Hen?' Shuff smiles at his own words. 'You want one of these birth certs?'

'No. I just mean it might be handy to have another ID. You never know what might happen. But yes, I'm thinking of getting one.'

'Or maybe,' Shuff downs three fingers in a sip, 'you just want to be somebody else.'

'No. I want to be me, but there might come a day when I need to be someone else. Know what I mean?'

'Peelers after you?'

'No.'

'Have they ever been?'

'No.'

'Someone after you?'

'No. No one.'

'You're twenty-six, mate. Bit late to be starting a life of crime.'

'That's not it. Doesn't matter.'

'Delaware.' A pause. 'Sounds like a man who rides a horse.'

'Yes. It's a state in America.'

'Everything's a state in America, fuck's sake.'

'Yes.'

Another minute passes and they begin their third pint. Shuff starts rolling a joint. Henry's heart skips a beat and comes back with a double.

'Bloody hell, Shuff – you can't do that here.' He feels his body tense, his mind momentarily sprint. He looks around.

Shuff flicks his eyes up as if Henry has lost the plot. Henry runs into his own head. He searches for a reason why Shuff might be able to freely roll a joint in a London bar. There's nothing there. No change of law on the news, no Amsterdam-style outlets opening up in the UK.

'Seriously,' he says, 98.89 per cent certain that this is illegal.

'Seriously?' asks Shuff, overemphasising, packing tobacco down onto the grassy flakes of drug, smiling. 'Don't be getting all serious on me now.'

'No. Look, I'm just pointing it out. We have to get to Romania and do this thing.'

'No one will arrest us or stab us or anything like that,' says Shuff. 'Don't you worry, big lad.'

'They obviously arrested you before.' Fuck Henry, why did you say that?

'Not exactly,' says Shuff, finishing his work. 'I handed myself in.'

Henry doesn't care about the details now. The illegal activity is causing him to sweat. This is an emergency but he doesn't have the strength to do anything but live it. His foot bounces where he stands.

And then, as he's licking the paper and forming a perfect cone, Shuff says: 'Do you want me to call you something else and see how it goes?'

'No,' says Henry, pissed off.

Shuff lights up, laughing peacefully as the curious witnesses to his crime look away. He shoots a blunt arrow of smoke from his nose as part of a tight laugh. It's got an unmistakable smell. The whole bar will know in seconds.

'If you speak with a Manchester accent instead of that British mishmash of yours,' he says, 'I'll call you Mr Delaware.'

'Piss off.'

Another shot of smoke from Shuff. 'Fuck's sake, Henry. You're only back in Blighty five minutes and you're going on about changing your ID. What the fuck, like?'

Henry says nothing. Then he says: 'Bollocks.' He shakes his head when Shuff offers him the joint. No thank you.

Shuff has a point, all right. The timing of his pathetic conversation is probably more than coincidence. Just being in England is being too close to that strange, fast child who could never run far enough from his own mind, too close to that dying woman, too close to a past of which he is ashamed. Henry feels he was never kind to people who were kind to him. Indeed, everyone was kind to him, his life in care was just that. He wants to hide from them all, from his stupid past, to be gone until he dies. He feels he will never have the strength to face up to who he was, to how he treated people who wanted only to help. He even hit his foster mother once, the one who's dying now, striking her on the face as she tried to comfort him. She had never held it against him. Only Henry had done that.

As the pair leave the pub, a stoned Shuff points at the barman. 'You're all right, big lad,' he says.

The barman nods. 'You too pal,' he says. He picks up the debris of Shuff's crime and bins it, head shaking.

Henry's going to ask Shuff about his tattoos. He decides this en route to the next bar, where Shuff's meeting his mates. He catches DD as Shuff holds open the door.

Says Shuff: 'Don't be bothered by these cunts.'

Henry feels himself having to catch his breath.

'Why? What's wrong with them?'

'Nothing,' says Shuff. 'It's you I'm thinking about. Just don't be bothered.'

There are five of them waiting in a private room off the main bar. They've already lined up dozens and dozens of drinks and asked the barman to close the hatch through which he had served the largest round Henry has ever seen. After Henry and Shuff's arrival, one of the men tucks his jacket along the bottom of the hatch, blocking a narrow gap into the bar. The same man closes the door when the group is complete, sealing them into a little square of their own. All five are delighted to see Shuff, and they all hug manfully in turn, slapping Shuff's broad back in the reunion. There's an emotional edge to the proceedings.

'Good to see you, big man,' says Gegeen. He turns to Henry and offers a hand. 'Gegeen. This is Birdie, Sam, Blackie and McFuck.' He might have said Mick Fuck, but it didn't matter.

Henry smiles as if he has met an interview panel, and shakes, attempting to copy the squeeze of each man who offers his hand. All are thick-skinned and sincere. 'I'm Henry. Nice to meet you.'

They wear open-necked shirts and jeans and look on the hard side of ordinary. You wouldn't insult any of them, whoever you are. Blackie's bald, but the rest have full heads of hair and look somehow more youthful than their fortyish years. Gegeen's had some damage done to an eye. They look like undercover policemen, with the confidence of knowing that they have the most clout on their side. The mood is subdued until Shuff lifts a glass of neat vodka. They gather round him in a circle and await his toast.

'Lads,' he says, raising his glass. 'Up yer arses.'

They all repeat it, except for a swiftly reddened Henry, and clink and drink. His head is swirling a little from all the beer. He feels nervous, a little excluded. Please don't go off on one. The men start laughing and ask about the flight to London and arrange seven seats in a circle. There's no table in the middle. Each man plants a mighty handful of drinks on the floor beside him, filling in the gaps between the chairs. Sam and bald Blackie cross their legs. Shuff settles himself, and spreads like the King.

Says McFuck: 'Shuff fucken Sheridan. It's been too long, mate.'

Shuff nods and smiles, his head tilts back as a large vodka pours into him. 'I tell you,' breathing out, 'it's fucken good to see youse. All of youse.'

'You too, mate, big time,' says Birdie. 'We met up last week and did nothing but talk about you, you cunt.'

Shuff laughs. McFuck asks Shuff how things are back in Belfast. Blackie, to Henry's right, turns to him.

'You're going to Romania or something?' he says, knocking back a double Irish whiskey. He reaches down and grabs another, passing one to Henry. Sam begins rolling a joint. Henry's cooling.

'Yes. I've got a business interest out there. I just need to see how it's going.'

'Sounds interesting,' says Blackie. 'Shuff's the muscle is he?'

'Yes,' says Henry, embarrassed. He feels dwarfed. 'You never know what might happen.'

'Oh aye,' says Blackie. 'Especially with fucken Shuff there.' He laughs. Henry doesn't. His stomach flips and he can feel himself blushing.

He says quietly, seriously, as if Blackie will be honest with him: 'Should I be worried?'

Blackie laughs: 'No, no, no. I'm only winding you up. If Shuff's on your side, you've already won. Trust me.'

'That's good to know.'

'Aye. He must reckon you're all right, bringing you here. He must've taken an interest in you. He does that with people sometimes.'

Henry likes the idea and downs a whiskey in quiet celebration. He hopes his age will have improved the taste, but it hasn't. Blackie tells Henry how none of the guys have seen Shuff since they left Belfast eighteen months ago. Henry asks if they ever go home, and Blackie shakes his head.

'No mate,' he says. 'We were all put out, you know. We'll go back one day.'

'Put out by who?'

'Paramilitaries and all that. Long story.'

'Right. Gosh. Was Shuff not put out?'

Blackie downs another drink and reaches below him. 'Oh aye,' he says. 'Well they asked him, but he politely told them to fuck off.'

'Really? Simple as that?'

Blackie nods. 'How long have you known him?'

'About a week.'

'Right. Well, he doesn't do things he doesn't want to do.'

'Okay.' A pause. 'Were you all threatened?'

'Aye. Point-of-a-gun job. Pain in the arse.'

Henry doesn't know how to advance this conversation. He thinks of the bar.

'Here, I'll get a round in.' He reaches to his back pocket.

'Don't bother,' says Blackie. 'We've a fund for these things. Just take any drink you want. No shortage.'

A large spliff comes Henry's way. He takes a draw and suppresses a cough before passing it to Blackie. Gegeen lifts a folder from a table behind him and opens it. He takes out leaves of paper and starts crumpling them up, his hard hands turning them into tiny parcels. He rolls them, one by one, onto the carpet in the middle of the circle. He sings: 'D-I-V-O-R-C-E,' and laughs.

Shuff, to Henry's left, rolls up his shirt sleeves. The tattoos cover every inch of his arms. They're little block capitals. They circle like a thousand skin-tight bracelets. Henry focuses. Shuff tells Gegeen how he's told a woman they both know that he's going to stamp the air out of her lungs. Henry works out the words.

PROVIDERANDDENIERPROVIDERANDDENIER PROVIDERANDDENIERPROVIDERANDDENIER PROVIDERANDDENIERPROVIDERANDDENIER, and on and on it goes.

'What does Provider and Denier mean?' he asks, swallowing whiskey, jerking at the flavour and turning to Blackie.

'Shuff.' A pause. 'It's some mad notion he took one day,' he says. 'It's from a book he read.'

'A book?'

'Aye,' says Blackie. 'Philosophy or something. He gets into some mad shit sometimes, so he does. I don't know.'

Gegeen looks over: 'The man who makes the rules, Henry. He's the Provider and Denier.' A sheaf of paper disappears into one of his fists.

Henry laughs nervously. The others are silent. Shuff turns to him and speaks.

'Just something I learned. Head stuff, you know.'

'Right,' says Henry, interested.

But Shuff stops it there. 'So, yiz fucken chickens, when are youse coming back to Belfast?'

Says Sam: 'I knew that was coming. It's not that simple, Shuff.'

Shuff snorts, looking at Henry again. 'It is that simple.'

They all shake their heads, as if Shuff doesn't know what they know.

Asks Henry: 'How long did the tattoos take, then?'

McFuck answers. 'One session. Two artists. Ten hours.'

Says Gegeen: 'I was there. When they were doing his back, it was like one of them massage tables. You know, where you put your face through? One of them. His girlfriend kept feeding him coke as he was lying there.'

They all laugh, and so does Henry. 'Well, they did a good job anyway.'

He wants to point out that Shuff must be nuts. His back too? The word vandalism passes through his mind.

Gegeen again, as the pile of crumpled paper in the centre grows: 'So, tell us about yourself, Henry.'

Henry's mind races, but to nowhere.

Gegeen again: 'Are you a religious man?'

Henry laughs. 'God, no. Not at all.' He doesn't know how to feel when no one says anything. 'Are you?' he nods, full of respect for the holy, at Gegeen.

'God, no,' and they all laugh, and so does Henry. 'I was once.'

'We all were once,' says Blackie, sinking a raw gin. Henry realises that all the drinks are neat spirits. 'Washed in the Blood of the Lamb, so we were.'

Henry's heard the expression before. 'Were you Saved? Isn't that what they call it?'

'Aye,' say Gegeen. 'Born Again.'

'Praise the Lord,' mocks Blackie.

Henry's baffled, but finds it easier now to relax as the conversation flies on, turning to London as Shuff is delivered information about where they're living and how their finances are. Sam tells how he's in with a Colombian, and Blackie says it won't be long until they know where he keeps his stash. McFuck knows a fearsome gang of Jamaican yardies and he's about to take them for everything they've got. The dispatches continue, simple, blurred, without either nonsense or detail, all aimed at Shuff. Henry slows down with the drinking. His head had been dizzy, now it's just heavy. An hour passes. The guys sink drink after drink, pints of raw spirits.

Gegeen stands up, burps and walks to a dimmer switch on the wall. The lights drop. Sam takes out his wallet and throws some money onto the paper pile. About £50 in all, Henry reckons, growing nervous. This isn't normal. The lights dip deeper as Blackie does the same thing, but with more cash. McFuck, the quietest of the bunch, throws in an envelope. Birdie empties out his wallet, dropping cards and cash and bits of paper. Shuff takes out his bag of weed and drops it in. Gegeen sits back down. Henry feels as if he should say nothing and just reach for his wallet, but his brain fights it. He's thrown his money in the air before, but he had his own reasons for that.

Says Shuff, a flat palm to Henry: 'Don't bother about it. It's just our thing.'

He leans forward and flicks his lighter. The fire catches what looks like a solicitor's letter and starts to take hold. Henry thinks he should lay off the drink altogether. He thinks he might need to keep his wits about him.

'Guys,' he says. 'You know this is a bit mad, don't you?'

They all laugh. 'Aye,' says Blackie, the flames flickering on his face in the blackness of the room, 'it's mad all right.'

Henry's legs tense and a foot starts to bounce. He can see the carpet catching fire. Yet the men sit comfortably, drinking hard and watching the flames eat up bills, cash, letters, credit cards and drugs.

'Bloody hell,' he says, scanning for alarms. 'I'm getting out of here.' The room is filling with smoke. 'Fellas, if you don't put that out, this whole place is going to burn.'

Shuff turns slowly from the fire, his head looking like a slow, solid block of steel in the confused foundry of flickering darkness. 'I keep telling you, Hen. You need to fucken relax, big lad.'

Henry points at the fire. 'That's a fire – in the middle of a room – in a pub! A bloody fire!' He stands up. The men look at each other, flicking their eyes as if Henry is a crazy fool. He wants to jump onto the flames.

'So what?' says Gegeen. 'What are you afraid of?'

Henry's dumbfounded. His heart is whacking off parts of his body that shouldn't feel its beat. It feels like it's pushing his entire interior around. 'I'm afraid of … I mean … what the bloody hell?'

Shuff turns to him again: 'Relax, Henry. No one is going to give us any shite. Don't be stressing yourself.'

Henry looks at the door and at Shuff, and chooses to sit back down. He looks at the faces around him and it reminds him of a camping trip. He decides he'll have to hang on and hope his heart doesn't give up on him.

'Anyone got any marshmallows?' he says, wondering if he's dreaming this mess up. It causes a few smiles deep in the thickening smoke. Birdie coughs.

Sure enough, the alarm goes off. A sprinkler kicks in as the men down the last of the drinks and collect their coats. A member of staff bursts through the door, red-faced, soaked and desperate, just as they begin to leave. He can't believe what he's seeing. Shuff pats him hard on the shoulder as he walks past and into the main bar.

'There's water in your vodka, big lad,' he says.

Sam laughs. People are screaming and drinking and gathering their things and heading for the door. A man wearing a tie grabs Henry's arm.

'Here,' he says, understandably furious at the fire in his bar, 'stop there.'

Blackie's balled fist cracks the man on the back of the head, knocking him forward, almost into Henry. Shuff's hand catches the man's face just in time and flings him back into Gegeen. Gegeen pushes him to the side, tumbling him onto a table loaded with abandoned glasses. Some of them break. There's blood. Henry feels scared, then protected, then scared as the man falls to the floor. His heart on overdrive, he walks out onto the street, planning a polite escape from these maniacs before he gets arrested.

He catches up with Shuff in the excited melee on the pavement outside. He feels curiously obliged to express some kind of thanks. 'Thanks,' he says, gasping. 'I think.'

'No problem, big lad.' Shuff looks only briefly at Henry. He looks like he's thinking. His wet white shirt reveals how the words really do run across every inch of his trunk, below the neckline. PROVIDERANDDENIER forever.

Henry wants to run, but he wants to ask and quiz and find things out. It's a moment of mental rush, a clattering ticker tape of questions which might have answers here and now. 'Come on, Shuff. What's the Provider and Denier thing?'

'I told you,' says Gegeen, flanking Henry's other side. 'The man who makes the rules. Provider and Denier.'

Shuff catches Henry's eye and shakes his head. 'It's fuck all, Henry.'

'Okay,' says Henry, 'but why did you get it tattooed?'

Gegeen: 'Shuff takes notions.'

Henry understands that. 'So do you make the rules?'

Shuff shakes his head: 'You're very fucken nosy, Hen.'

'Sorry. I'm not normally. Just interested. I mean, it all seems a bit crazy to me.'

Shuff nods. 'I suppose.' A pause. 'I read this book. Philosophy stuff. Guy from Belfast. He came up with the Provider and Denier thing. I met him and all. Interesting guy, you know.'

Henry senses there's something more to this. 'So you had his words tattooed all over you? You must have loved them.'

'Aye. I just met this tattooist one day. I was drunk, and that was that.'

Gegeen looks Shuff's way. 'It's kind of about all of us.' He tries to catch Shuff's eye. 'We all read the book.'

Shuff keeps walking, eyes ahead: 'Then why did you go, Geg? I stayed, you went. Who was making the rules then?'

Gegeen focuses back on the road, told off. 'It'll be all right, Shuff,' he says.

They walk for a while, wide streets, broad buildings, shiny brass plaques. Shuff catches Henry's eye: 'You've a fucked up conscience, haven't you Henry?'

It was an out-of-the-blue, curious question, but a well-informed one. Henry's conscience has more firepower than the United States.

'Fucked up?' he says. A pause. 'Well, it keeps itself busy.' Shuff has almost stunned him.

'It's holding you back.' Shuff had said it with feeling. 'You should read that book.'

'Why?'

'Because it'll sort your head out.'

Gegeen: 'Do you believe in God at all, Henry?'

'No. Atheist. Or agnostic.'

Gegeen laughs: 'Doubt? Now there's a philosophy.' He's sarcastic.

'Yes.' Henry can't stand the idea of being watched by a God.

Says Shuff: 'Why are you so scared, big lad?'

Henry feels as if he's shrinking: 'Scared? I'm not.'

'You are. You're fucken terrified all the time. That's why we're going to fucken Romania together in the first place.'

'I just try to keep in the right, that's all.'

Shuff says nothing for a moment. Henry is embarrassed, but he does wonder where the conversation will take him. Shuff knows this. He can read Henry's sincere curiosity, his need to resolve.

He says: 'Your conscience rules you, Hen. You should tell it to fuck off. It's holding you back.'

Henry nods. 'Yes. But if your conscience is clear then you've nothing to worry about.'

'No, you're not listening,' says Shuff.

'I am,' says Henry. 'Your conscience doesn't bother you. That's what you said.'

Shuff shakes his head. 'No. I'm saying you don't need a conscience. It's a pain in the arse. When you get rid of it, nothing bothers you any more.' He looks at Henry. 'There's no one watching. You're free.'

Henry's confused. 'But there's right and wrong.'

'No there's not.'

'There is.'

'Why? Why worry if there's no God to worry about?'

Henry says nothing for a moment. Gegeen looks his way, just to see what Henry is doing with his face.

'So that's it,' says Henry. 'This is your big philosophy? No right or wrong?'

'My philosophy is to kill the conscience and move on.'

Says Gegeen: 'You can crack it, Henry. Just keep pushing it. Sooner or later, it'll go. You can kill it.'

Henry laughs. 'That wouldn't work.'

Gegeen: 'It works. Read that book. *The Last Door*.'

'*The Last Door?*' says Henry.

'Aye,' says Shuff. 'It's got that stuff about Providers and Deniers in it. It's about finding the right door in the head and opening it. Escaping, you know.'

Henry likes the phrase, The Last Door. It hits a button, clicks a latch in his trap-doored mind. 'The Last Door. What happens after that?'

Shuff shrugs. 'You feel fucken grand, Hen, that's what happens.'

Gegeen: 'After you go through the Door, you get rich. You realise you own anything you want to own.'

Henry is confused: 'What do you mean?'

Gegeen: 'No conscience, no rules, clear head. The world's all yours when you think like that. There's no limits on you. Think about it.'

Henry nods. He's not sure if he's scared now, or just mystified. The men are like some kind of fundamentalist cult, some kind of twisted communists.

'And you're saying that's a good thing to learn?'

'We are,' says Gegeen. 'It's a way to do things. Everyone needs a way to do things.'

Henry nods again. 'And you don't care who owns the things you want?'

Shuff laughs: 'No, Hen. We don't care. We never did. We were probably heading for that fucking Door anyway, only we didn't know it.'

Gegeen laughs: 'Aye. We'd some mad fucken times, all right.'

'It sounds crazy,' says Henry. 'You sound like nihilists.'

Neither Shuff nor Gegeen like the word. Shuff thinks it's got something to do with losing.

'Whatever. But it works,' says Gegeen.

'So that's what you do? Steal things?'

Gegeen burps: 'We take what we know is our own.'

Henry thinks for a moment. 'So do any of you have jobs?'

Gegeen: 'No need, mate. The only work we do is to keep it going. But Shuff's left the company.'

Shuff looks at him: 'Geg, you're the cunt who couldn't take it any more.'

'Fuck that, Shuff. I'd no choice. You know how it was. You should have come to London.'

'Fuck that,' says Shuff. 'You were beat. You're all fucken Champagne Warmers to me. You wrecked the party.'

Henry asks: 'How do Geg and the rest of them go back to Belfast then, if they're under threat?'

Shuff shakes his head: 'The same way you would. On a fucken plane.'

They walk onto Sloane Street. A huge silence surrounds them. Blackie, Sam, Birdie and McFuck are laughing at something behind.

'What did you burn the money for?' Henry feels emboldened enough, drunk enough, to ask odd questions of men who have unusual answers.

'Just pushing ourselves,' says Gegeen. 'Listen, is there anything you want to do, Henry?' asks Gegeen. 'You know, anything you want?'

'Not really. I don't want to burn my money, though.'

'Listen to the man,' says Shuff. 'Is there anything you want?'

'No.'

Gegeen: 'Anything you want to do that you think you can't? Anything at all? Come on – give yourself a push.'

'You mean like nick something?'

'Could be,' says Shuff, knocking into the side of a man walking towards him.

'I don't understand,' says Henry.

'Then you're not living, big lad,' says Shuff. 'You're in a wee fucken box, so you are.'

Henry resents that: 'I'm not going to start doing what you do. I mean, you can't go round just doing what you want. I mean, what about the cops and all?'

Gegeen: 'What about car accidents and cancer and AIDS and lightning? You can't fucken hide, Henry. You just gotta get on with it before you die.' A pause. 'And good alibis go a long way too.' Gegeen smiles at that one.

Henry thinks of his foster mother and the lumps scattered through her centre like mines on slow release.

'All I can think of ... Well, I want to feel better about something.' There's silence. He continues, unsure if he will sound ridiculous. 'A woman I know who's dying,' he says. 'I wish I could clear it up in my head, that's all. Is there a way to clear things like that up?'

'Aye, that's an easy one,' says Shuff. He stops. They're outside the bar he and Henry were in earlier. A fire engine flies by, sirens wailing, blue lights bashing the glass walls of the street. 'Just forget the fucken bitch.' A pause. 'Now, if you're a businessman then you must worry about money, right?'

Henry's startled. He's not sure what Shuff said after calling his foster mother a bitch.

Shuff takes Henry's eyes and points. 'Henry. Go in there and get that barman's ring. It'd be worth a few hundred.'

'What?' There's no chance of him doing that. Had Shuff really called her a bitch? 'Did you ...,' he said. 'Did you mean steal his ring?'

Shuff smiles. 'Yep. Take it. It's yours.'

'No way.' He thinks how anything could happen to him whether he does it or not. These guys could do anything at all right now. They've said as much, done as much.

Gegeen laughs: 'Go on there, Henry. What are you afraid of?'

'Getting hit,' Henry admits. 'You see the size of that guy?'

Gegeen laughs again, as if that's not worth worrying about. If only Gegeen lived in Henry's lesser body and unsettled mind, he'd understand. The others arrive at the scene and stop.

Gegeen, rocking ever so slightly on his feet, points at Shuff. 'You see this man? We'd never have done fuck all without him. He's no fear. No fear at all. He hasn't got the gene. You'll learn more from Shuff Sheridan than you'll ever learn from anyone.'

Blackie nods: 'Biggest man in Belfast, Henry. Biggest man in the whole fucken world. We've all seen it.'

Birdie agrees: 'No doubt about it.'

McFuck: 'That's why he's the right man for this Romania thing. Fucken dodgy out there.'

Shuff chips in: 'Me granda was Russian. Communist as fuck. I'm very proud of that.'

A thought barges through Henry. 'You just want the guy's ring because you know he's Catholic.' He feels it's a dangerous thing to say. 'You just want to hit him or something.' His words are slurred.

'No,' says Shuff. 'Get a fucken grip on the situation, Hen. Sure Blackie's a Catholic. Big IRA family too.'

'That's right,' says Blackie. 'Republican as fuck. Me uncle killed a cousin of Shuff's. A peeler.'

'S'right,' says Shuff. 'Shot the cunt in the face.'

Henry's head shakes fast. 'Look, I don't want the bloody ring.' He just wants to get some sleep now. He tells himself to wise up, that this is fucked up and won't get any better.

'All right then,' says Shuff, turning to walk on. 'Fuck it.'

'I want the ring,' says Gegeen. Shuff stops. He looks around at the stony faces. Gegeen points a finger: 'And I want Shuff to get it.'

Shuff nods. Henry looks into the bar, at the man from County Fermanagh chatting to a punter. His heart starts to pound again. He feels bad already about what's going to happen. Shuff pushes the door. Henry looks around, terrified, baffled by this night.

Inside, Shuff approaches the bar. The barman nods, recognising him from before. 'Back for more?' he says.

Shuff smiles: 'You've one chance, big lad. One chance. Gimme the ring.'

The barman smiles, almost laughs, looking at his finger: 'What? Away on.' He looks out the window and sees an audience staring his way. Shuff walks to the end of the bar and flips up the hatch.

'Here now, boy,' says the barman, 'get away to fuck.' He reaches under the bar and grabs a half-size, aluminium baseball bat. The punters look, whispering, unclear. Gegeen spits on the street. Henry doesn't know if he wants to look. What if Shuff gets hurt? He looks.

The punters fall silent. A man at the bar pulls back on his stool, looking around for answers. The barman takes a proud stance and gets ready to swing.

'I'll fucken clock you,' he says, serious as death.

Shuff turns to his right and grips the cash register. He growls as he pulls it back, lifting it up, its lights a whirr of confusion, its plug jerked out of the wall. 'You had your chance,' he says, breathing out, 'stupid fucker.'

The man swings, catching Shuff's left hand as the till rises up in front of him. It's meaningless. He swings at Shuff's belly. The till is thrust into his face, smashing him back against the bar, thudding him against oddly named beer taps. Shuff drives the till further, like pushing a car, lifting the man from his feet, pouring booze and breaking a Fermanagh collarbone with the force. He pulls the till back and rams it again. Screams ring out, a woman dials a number on a mobile with a shaking finger, people scatter to everywhere but the door. The barman holds his hands out, shaking, not able to remember which one his wedding ring is on. Shuff drops the till. The drawer flies open as it hits the ground, cash bursting onto the scene like a small bomb in a small bank. Shuff grabs the ring, kneeing the man in the stomach as he tugs it from his finger, stealing a thick strip of skin as it comes off.

The path Shuff takes as he leaves the pub is far wider than it was when he came in. Standing, shaking customers form a broad, nervous tunnel. Shuff opens the door and hands the ring to Gegeen. The door closes. Gegeen shakes the skin from it and slips it onto a finger.

'You see how it works, Henry?' he says, as if there had been a wonderful revelation. Henry has no response, no movement. Gegeen turns: 'Here, Shuff,' he says, 'Nice to see you back.'

Shuff nods once, the way a hero nods. 'Aye,' he says. 'Come on to fuck. I need a drink.'

Henry's legs wobble as he starts walking again, lifting them like dead weights. It feels like he's in a dream, like he's trapped and unable to escape. He looks all around, but witnesses look away when they see his eyes. He tries to keep up with the others, to hide among them in the eye of the storm. His stomach jerks, his mind is blank, as if the horror image of what he has just seen has punched him in the gut. A sour vomit flavour swirls inside his mouth and he gasps, bending over, still walking, waiting to be sick amid the chirpy, mad voices of these men. He is too weak to speak, too distressed to focus, too sick to think.

In the corner of his eye, he can see Gegeen smiling and holding out the ring. Henry's mouth stays wide, awaiting illness, as Gegeen polishes the blood from its heart and crown. Henry had known the ring meant more than just price, that the barman was being robbed of something special. But he can't remember thinking that now, nor remember anything as he turns his head. There is a silence, as if he has been struck deaf after dumb, after his mind has been wiped. And then, just loud enough to hear, some kind of crackling little voice from somewhere tells him that the ring could have been his. He puts the words out of his mind, terrified at how bad they are, trying to go blank again. Had he said them himself? He doesn't know. But it would not have been a case of taking what he knew was his own. It would not.

The men want to drink, screw, steal hard drugs and probably have a fight with anyone in London, because they will not lose. When Henry gathers himself, all he wants to do is go back to his hotel, to be alone, to throw in any towel he can get, to give in to the aftershock of the most violently pointless thing he has ever seen. Shuff tells him he's missing out, but he only wants to lie in bed and be free to absorb and process and sleep and recover and to get the hell away from these men.

He takes a black taxi, arrives with a white face, goes to his dark room. The light comes on for less than a minute before it's off again and Henry is in bed, covers pulled tight around him. This thing, this chemical disorder, really could rise again, he thinks. He hasn't felt its full power since his teens. The long, massive moods that pitched his brain against itself, consumed him with self-hatred and guilt and insisted on isolation are a memory, but still a threat. Shadows lurk and shadows rise. They rose the other day at a pointless, time-killing language lecture, but only a little bit for a little while, only because of all the shit going on. He wonders if his whole view of this night has been coloured by his illness, if it has come back in its wildest fashion yet, making things up, showing him that he's more out of touch with things that are right than he's ever been, throwing blood and gold and screams into his path.

He wishes he was someone else now. Someone else would get up and leave, go far away from Shuff Sheridan. No one else would stay with this madman, or travel with him, or try to be his friend. Someone else would go up north to the bedside of that dying lady who knew how to love yet contain extraordinary stillness and crazy, rudderless energy. And someone else would go and find Alina, and tell her he wanted her and marry her and give her everything.

He imagines his head, falling, severed from his body, dropping down through black air. Shots ring out, pounding bullets into it, face creasing with the agony of the violent lead thumping into his brain. It tumbles on and on, is shot more and more. He squeezes his eyes with the pain. He opens them only to see the bruised blackness of his own fist punching him in the face again and again. He doesn't know when he fell asleep, blood dripping from his nose onto the thick white sheets. He can't think now, wrapped up, comatose, but if he could he'd think the one thing he really wants is never to wake up.

9

Two weeks ago, a plane neatly tucked in its wheels above London and made for Bucharest, the grand capital of old Romania. On board was a group of young volunteers bound for Iasi on a mission to redecorate a grim orphanage, a home to infected children. All its residents were HIV-positive, tragic time bombs, poisoned before they reached life. The orphanage was a stone, grey place where it always felt like winter, its thick walls exuding nothing but cold. The volunteers knew they were all going to have a moving experience of some kind, and their spirits were high shields against the unknown sights that lay ahead. They had adopted a holiday spirit, because they didn't know what other spirit to adopt. They had a drink and a laugh on the plane and talked about the price of alcohol in Romania. They had all either heard or imagined it was dirt cheap.

On the same plane sat a man who calls himself GADAKA, but only when online. His mission could not have made more of a contrast. As he sat sipping a drink and flicking through the in-flight magazine, he felt entirely certain that he was going to have one of the most dazzlingly sordid adventures of his life. He was able to control his excitement with remarkable aplomb, and he liked himself for it.

He imagined Alina would be nervous when she met him, but he knew he would calm her with his full smile and soft words. Pacification was such a breeze, he often felt. He grew hard on the plane, the words on the page blurring as his mind flicked through the images he had purchased and memorised to help him thrive.

He dozed off a little, his head full of the thoughts he loved more truly than anything else in the world. He remembered his wife's weeping face as he left, as he told her not to worry about the bills and the blacklistings because he was going on a trip that would solve all their problems. She kissed him, he patted the heads of his daughter and son, and he left. They waved him farewell, all hoping that this time he would return home with the certain knowledge that he would be able to beat the wolf back from the door. GADAKA knew he would be able to do nothing of the sort, but now it was time to really not care about all that again. The cost of his trip would be a small price to pay for the precious ecstasy he was about to unleash on himself.

One of the volunteers, a short-haired gothic sixteen-year-old called Judy, knocked his arm by accident as she passed him on her way to the toilet.

'Sorry,' she said, smiling.

'No problem,' he said, sitting up straight and pulling his arm in.

A tall man sitting beside him whispered: 'I think some of them are drinking.'

GADAKA nodded and rubbed his stubble: 'Bloody airlines.'

The erection was settling itself now, the images fading from his mind as he thought of the practicalities of landing and making his way to the train for Iasi. It would be a trip of some seven hours from Bucharest, and he hoped nobody would bother him. He had no time for Romanians, beyond those females he had wooed. He hadn't been to Iasi before and looked forward to the sights and to a rested, peaceful arrival. The remains of his erection disappeared and his balls began to gently throb.

He thought of the teenage couple who had tricked him in a Cambodian hotel last year, and attacked his naked testicles as he prepared to have his way. The girl had thick and jagged dirty nails. She had grabbed him from below and behind, dragging him naked and backwards, squeezing him so hard that he was fully unable to fight. They had scarpered from the hotel like rats, his wallet and clothes in their hands, and he had never seen them again. Every erection these days was accompanied by an ache. It could be during or after, but the ache would always present itself, making him sometimes walk as if he had a limp. If only he could have that Cambodian afternoon over again, he often thought. Those little fuckers would have been given something to think about. But then again, time is the one thing a man can't toy with.

He breathed in as the thought struck him that Alina might try the same thing. And he breathed out in the certain knowledge that this wouldn't happen. He knew how to do everything now. Once bitten, twice wise.

In England, a woman was consoling herself with the thought that deserving children were benefiting from her charity. Old Matilda liked to isolate her thoughts and focus, meditating on the smiling faces that would greet the volunteers when they arrived with time, energy and big, full hearts, all set to make a difference to beautiful, terrible little lives. She had been to Iasi and seen the twisted legacy of the Ceausescu regime, that fearsome club which had tried to help only itself by plunging its people into a violent era of shortages. It had raided its own assets and, while the rational world united in the war against AIDS, it had emptied operating theatres and pumped untested, infected blood into pregnant bodies and tiny arms. It hushed, ferociously, anyone who was unpatriotic enough to so much as whisper how wrong it was, to so much as hint that

AIDS could be a problem in Romania. Matilda could imagine no greater evil than the silent slaughter of the innocents in a manner which caused them to scar, lose weight, grow ill and weak, to suffer and die so horribly, and so young. It forced on her more anger than she was able to accept.

She had been to the orphanage. She'd had her hands cleansed of potential infectants by a nurse who had gently killed her own dog because she could not afford to feed it. Then Matilda met some of the tens of thousands of victims of the Monster's whim, of the poisoned bloodlines still running through a society trying to stand. She first went upstairs to see the HIV kids, the happy little tykes who didn't always know they were sick. She played on the carpet with them, kissed and hugged them and showed them the simple mystery of removing a thumb. The staff had the youngsters perform a little song and dance for her, and she felt the tears well up in her clear brown eyes as they sang in wandering, simple English for her own entertainment. She knew her God was with her, and all through the room, as she adored all she saw.

A little black-haired boy with bruises and wounds developing on his body showed her a montage of pictures on a wall. They were polaroids of children who had lived in that room, but who had been moved downstairs for reasons the little boy didn't understand. He knew nothing of the poison in his blood. The older orphans suspected something, but had no one who would confirm or deny the rumours about a deadly virus that brought them to this place. She stroked the little boy's shiny hair as he told her, all happy and fun, about his friends. He pointed to pictures of Gregor, of Elena, of Tiberiu and Lucia. Again Matilda fought back the tears, terrified she would cause a conflict of emotion, an upset in the child's pure, sick heart.

She hugged and kissed them all again as the nurse took her downstairs, pulse pounding, to the quiet, dark place where the children go when they develop full-blown AIDS, where they go to die. The smell of chemicals filled her as she met each of them, lifting up little hands too weak to move and kissing little faces too thin to smile. It was there, when she saw dying little Elena from the picture upstairs, that she began to weep. She smiled and smiled as she left the room, and when she was out of view of the children, she cried up every tear she had. She collapsed against a wall and a nurse brought her a glass of water. She bowed in prayer and pleaded, even demanded of her God, that the children suffer no more. She left Romania the next day, having posed for a picture as she delivered the money she had raised to a woman she would have trusted with her life. She left part of her soul in that death room in Iasi, and prayed for it and the children every waking hour of every day since. She even prayed in her dreams, and she always woke up tired.

Matilda had raised much more money in the intervening years, working like a saint to give something to the innocents cursed by that man who would have lied to the world had it ever bothered asking him what the hell he was doing. Now she had funded the volunteers, sending them out with money and a dream to help make the orphanage a place where dying children go to live, not where living children go to die. She had given the cash to a girl called Judy, a lovely bright child whom she knew would not let her down, and told her to hide it from every official, from every clerk, from everyone. She told her to give it only to the woman at the orphanage in Iasi. It would be something, she thought, but she wished to God she could do more.

Now she had come to the end of her days. The cancer which ate away inside her, she knew, was God's forewarning and she would answer when he was ready to call. She would miss her life and miss feeling the endless, unbreakable, powerful mother's love for all the world's children with which she had been blessed. She was sorry she wouldn't see her troubled little Henry before she was called home, but she knew in her heart this was because he must be on a more worthy mission, as was God's great plan. She hoped he had forgiven himself for stealing from her, for hitting her, for the crimes he had committed against her as she tried to give him the peace he had so badly needed. She hoped he had already found a spiritual guidance, a path which she had found and walked in her later years.

Matilda Sender felt selfish now that she had a little happiness in her tired heart, and a little joy that she was going forth into Paradise, into the magnificent presence of her Lord. She felt a little guilty that she was glad Nicolae Ceausescu was in Hell, and asked for forgiveness for these sinful thoughts in her final moments.

10

The door opens. Someone takes several careful steps to their spot. A cigarette packet is unwrapped. A cigarette is lit.

'Fuck's sake,' says Rosie, to herself.

Della joins, pulling the door behind. It takes three whacks to get it to fit into its frame. 'Fuck's sake,' says Della. 'Fucken door's a cunt.'

Rosie tuts. 'It's your fault it's fucked. Don't moan at me.'

'I'm nat moanin at you.'

'Yar.'

'Nat. It's nat my fault anyway.'

'Fucken is. Sure Muck shat the fucken thing, the looper.'

'Fuck up.'

'Near killed us, so he did.'

'Didn't. He only shat the tap of it.'

'What difference does that make?'

'HE COULDN'T HAVE SHAT US. WE'RE SMALL.'

Rosie tuts again. 'What if we'd been standin on a chair?'

'What the fuck would we be standin on a chair for?'

'FIXIN A LIGHT.'

'Wise up.' Della folds her arms and flicks hard and fast at her cigarette. 'He only wanted to shoot NAILER and then he thought about shootin Daddy.'

'Why didn't he just call at the door then? Like normal people?'

'Fuck up. I don't want Daddy shat anyway.'

Rosie tuts. 'Then why didn't you stap him?'

'I was onie out of hospital. I didn't know what was goin on with all the drugs they'd give me. I was fucken depressed.'

'How'd ya explain Muck then?'

'He was onie actin the ballix.'

'The ballix?'

'HE WAS ANGRY. He knows Daddy hates him. Sure he hates Charlie too.'

'Not like Muck. Daddy'll kill him one day.'

'He'll nat.'

'If he finds out you're still with him, he will.'

'HE'LL NAT FIND OUT THEN.'

'So when's he gettin this car? Or is it gonna be one of them new invisible ones?'

'He's nat gat it yet, right.'

'He's nat gat nathin.'

'Aye right.'

Della's been crying. Earlier she told Rosie she'd accidentally wiped her eyes with a handkerchief that had been used to wipe up a puddle of spicy sauce on the sideboard. It was a lie. Her eyes are red. She hurts.

'You cryin again?'

'It's that sauce. And nigh the sun's in me eyes.'

Rosie tuts. 'Me fucken arse. You need to move on, love. Start livin again. When's daddy comin home?'

'How the fuck do I know?'

'Does Mummy know?'

'HOW THE FUCK DO I KNOW?'

Rosie tuts. 'Do you think he'll bring us somethin back?'

'Hang on till I check me fucken crystal ball.'

Rosie tuts. 'I'm onie fucken chattin. Don't be so fucken humpy.'

'The peelers wanna speak to him again. That woman toal Mummy they did.'

'Waste of time. Do they want Daddy to solve the case or somethin? They couldn't find a fucken haystack in a needle.'

'Aye. They didn't even find me fucken Es in the bedroom.'

'Aye, thank fuck.'

'Anno.'

'Here, I hear your Charlie's Da's got a dog nigh.'

Rosie tuts. 'Aye. One of them big-headed scary ones, so it is.'

Della tuts. 'For fightin?'

'Aye.'

'I fucken hate that. What do they have to do that for?'

'For money. What the fuck do you think? Milky Bars?'

'It's sick.'

'Anno. But he has to get money from somewhere.'

'It's sick as fuck.'

'You didn't say it was sick when we'd NAILER.'

'I THOUGHT IT WAS A PET.'

'Some fucken pet. It chewed half that door off. Fucken thing came home with no ears one night.'

'Anno. He never even fed it.'

'You're supposed to keep them hungry, so yar.'

Della tuts. 'I mind it started runnin into that wall and the door and all one day. It barked at the sun and all. Fucken bonkers, so it was.'

'Aye, well Muck sorted all that out when he took the head staggers that night. Fucken wanker. Why did he fucken do that anyway?'

'Dunno. To get at Daddy for hatin him and slappin him that time. I don't like all that fightin.'

'Daddy's just protective.'

'He's just nuts. Muck did nathin.'

'He tried to kill him and then hit him in the nuts with a sledgehammer.'

'THAT WAS AFTER,' Della spits.

'Fuck's sake.' Rosie spits. 'Daddy toal Mummy he's gonna come back with loads of money.'

'Fuck's sake. His head's full of shite.'

'Anno. Where's Mummy?'

'Dunno.'

'She was cryin last night.'

'Why?'

'Daddy's balls.'

'Fuck off.'

'It's true. When she was drunk on the phone she was sayin to Marcie Boyle his balls aren't workin no more.'

Della tuts. 'Well, he's too old to be usin them nigh anyway.'

'She says his stuff's gone all watery and it hurts him to get it out.'

'Good. I don't want another sister or brother or nathin.'

'Not even a wee Robert?'

'You're a mean bitch, Rosie.'

'I'm nat.' She is.

'Muck's took on more work, so he has.'

'To pay for the big runaway?'

'Fuck up.'

'Unclench your fucken hole.'

Two more cigarettes are ignited at the same time. Another round of high-speed smoking begins. Della wants to ask her only sister a question. She hates to do it, but feels Rosie might know the answer.

'What's a lowbrow?'

'Wha?'

'A lowbrow?'

'Dunno. Why?'

'See, Muck's fixin jewellery in this other place nigh, part-time.'

'Fucken Tiffany's, no doubt.'

'No. Gerry's. Gerry's Jewels. Where's Tiffany's?'

'Forget it, you dozy bitch.'

Della tuts. 'Fuck up. At least Muck works.'

'Charlie works.'

'I didn't know LYIN DOWN was a job.'

'Fuck you.' A pause. 'I don't know what lowbrow is. Maybe it's low eyebrows or somethin.'

'Nah, couldn't be that.'

'Is it one of them battled beers from Germany?'

'Nah. It's nat that.'

'What're you on about, fucken lowbrow?'

'I'm tryin to tell ya. Muck's trumpet teacher asked him where he worked and all, and then said his bling was lowbrow.'

'Right. I dunno.'

'He said it was cheap, like. Then he said it was lowbrow.'

'Right. What did Muck say?'

'Said what did he mean and the guy just said nathin. Then he said Muck was lowbrow too and Muck still didn't know what he meant.'

'He's nat gat low brows.'

'Nah. I don't know. Muck's gonna look it up. If it's bad he's going to go back and punch the cunt.'

'Me arse. He'd never do nathin like that. Big soft shite, so he is.'

'Anno. The other guy in the class just says yer man's always like that. Cheeky and all. If lowbrow's cheeky, like.'

'Aye. I fucken hate teachers and bosses and all. Fucken orderin you about all the time.'

'That's what Daddy says.'

'Anno, it's true.'

'Did you hear him shoutin out here the other night?'

'No. Was he?'

'Aye. Mummy said he was in the yard shoutin at himself and makin a racket.'

'Fuck knows. Fucken eejit.'
'Aye.'
'Come on to fuck, Della. I want me breakfast.'
'Aye.'

Frank's second night had been pretty restless. His limbs are numb. The deadness makes him feel heavy and useless. Blankness is within him and around him. He misses not having the sun to colour things in each day.

He's fairly sure he hasn't passed anything in something like twenty-four hours and he's thirstier than he's ever been. His hands feel like they don't belong to him, feeling almost nothing that they touch. His eyes hurt when he closes them, and they hurt when they open, and hurt whether they are open or closed. His head is a constant scream of agony, like a permanent ache in every inch of his brain. His sense of smell has left him and he can't feel himself breathe. I would have turned ninety-two next week, he thinks from nowhere. Happy Birthday.

He'd taken some joy at hearing the girls enter the arena again, their shrill alarm reminding him that he knew them from before. Their fiery drip-feed was his only stimulation, beyond the elements and the random shouts of the city. He liked the opening of the door and the short, foul escape which followed. He's sure now he heard them more clearly today than yesterday, and thinks that maybe his body is only shutting down the non-essential services. He feels that his hearing is actually improving, his brain whirring a little more. It's amazing what the body can do, he thinks.

They seemed nice, the crazy smokers. He felt that they had a coarse honesty, that they had not grown up in an environment in which it was thought best to contain one's own point of view. He was sure they were close, that they were connected, and that their relationship was maintained by an extreme emotion which they would miss should they be parted. He thought too of Della and her dreams of leaving, and he understood. He just wasn't sure why there was such an urgency to it, why it was on both their minds at least once a day, why it felt like it was imminent. Rosie was constantly trying to rubbish this dream. She too probably felt that it might just become reality soon, and she would lose her loud friend to the world. Francis M.N. Cleary thinks through it all.

He closes his right thumb and forefinger together, feeling a light touch fight back against the heavy numbness. After some hard work, he manages to get some blood flowing and can work his hand like a pincer. It has little strength. He puts it onto the damp collar of his old blue and white striped pyjama top and gently begins to feel. It will be difficult, but after a time he's sure he's managed to get the collar between his pincers, and he runs the pads of thumb and finger up and down. He brings his hand to the edge so that if he should grip, he would seize just a couple of millimetres of cloth, and he runs it up and down again. He concentrates intensely on what he can sense, willing himself to put his last reserves of life into the nerves on his hand, pleading with himself to just be able to feel what he's doing, but resigns himself to senselessness. After a time, he just grips, hoping to get lucky. He closes his finger and thumb. Very gently, he pulls. A little thread is drawn from its home, and as he holds his hand up to the light, his eyes burning, he can just make out that it's there – that it's short – but it's there. It's about four inches long. He places it very carefully onto his immobile forehead and goes back to where he was, searching blindly for another end of weightless stitch with a hand almost bereft of feeling. There's a lot of work to do.

As the day went on, he groped and gripped, finding and gathering little thread after little thread, aching and fading, burning and breaking. He kept wanting to give up, but after a rest he would always start again. He just couldn't stop, he couldn't call it off. He knew it was theoretically possible, and that was enough to keep telling himself over and over again that it could be done. Do something useful, Frank, he told himself. It's about time you did something useful.

My dear old friend,

Detective Sergeant Ryan rang to say that he had informed Social Services that I was a danger to myself. I tried to convince him that I was in fact a danger to society, but he wouldn't have it. He said I was a pain in the arse of society, but not a danger to it. He cursed about twenty times on the phone. I think he's losing the plot. He said he had decided against prosecuting for wasting police time because he believed Social Services could teach me a lesson more effectively than he could.

The Fan shoved me into the kerb, I think by accident. I met him outside his house on Monday and said I'd claimed responsibility for his latest offerings, and he slapped me on the shoulder as he laughed. This was enough to almost knock me over. He said then that I shouldn't take all the blame, that he wanted some responsibility for his own actions. A man called out to him for slapping me so hard, and he threatened to kill the man. Nothing came of it. I rang the station and said I'd made a threat to kill a man. Nothing came of that either. I AM IN TORMENT.

He still likes me, my Fan. He still likes to hear me talk and ponder life and death and doors. I can always get him to tell me what he's been up to. He likes to tell tales, to let his demons out of his big head.

My little dog has been becoming yet more distant and staying away for longer and longer periods of time. He looks at me strangely and even growls occasionally, but this only encourages me to do the same. Perhaps he thinks I'm taking over his role. He left early this morning after his breakfast. I hope he comes back.

The students' union people wrote. Their president invited me to the end of term party. They think I'm some kind of mad mascot. I wrote back and said I could not go because I had planned a brutal crime for that same afternoon. I'm sure they understand. I don't expect to hear from anyone there again. They're nice people. They do good things. I wish I'd never polluted their space with M.N..

Regards, old friend,

Francis Cleary

11

A man approaches Henry at the train station in Iasi to ask if he needs a taxi. He moves in a little too close for comfort, causing Henry to think he's either trying to intimidate him into accepting his offer, snatch his wallet or stab him. Henry looks behind, hoping to see the massively hungover, bloodshot face of Shuff Sheridan, but it isn't there. By the time he turns back again, Shuff is standing with his arm tight around the taxi driver's shoulder like they're old buddies.

'All right, Hen?' asks Shuff. The Romanian's incensed, trying to pull away from the powerful grip which has locked him close to Shuff's body. Shuff tells the man to be still, and Henry answers that he's fine, thanks. Shuff lets the man go and he curses, spits and walks quickly away.

'I'm working now, Henry,' says Shuff. 'I'm all yours, big lad.' Henry smiles.

His night of fitful sleep had led to a morning of planning, of attempted escape, but it had come to nothing more than five coffees and an episode of violent discharge in a hotel toilet. He wasn't sure if courage had once again failed him and blocked him from leaving the hotel without Shuff, in case he caught him. And he wasn't sure if courage had seized him, stopped him and instead driven him forwards, onwards to Romania, to Alina's city, no matter what. He had been shaking and blinking when he had met Shuff again, but Shuff had touched his arm and told him that everything was okay, that it was all going to work out. Shuff had this morning stepped into the no-man's-land of Henry's mind, into its numb neutrality, and somehow told him he would stand by his side. Shuff Sheridan, bleary-eyed from drink and lack of sleep, had quietly led the way and taken Henry from the hotel to the taxi, and to their flight from London to Romania.

Shuff had slept for most of the seven-hour train journey from Bucharest, occasionally shouting something which sounded like *fucken will ye* or maybe *fucken kill ye*, and farting like an ox. Henry stayed awake throughout, sometimes just staring at Shuff, sometimes planning to get off at stops along the way, sometimes snatching glances at the man and woman who had joined their rundown compartment. The couple ate a neat packed lunch and whispered in smooth-edged Romanian to each other about a friend in Bucharest. 'Dah,' they said, time and time again. The word begins with a tiny hum. Mmdah = yes. It's the real, live, whirling sound of an Italian relative, the true Romance language of the East. Henry liked its soft familiarity. The words relaxed him. He suspected the couple might be talking about Shuff's commotions. He was glad they didn't know that the two men were together.

They arrived, the couple alighting quickly, and Henry could not wake Shuff without standing on his foot. He had pushed his arm, called his name and poked a finger gingerly into a podgy cheek, but it came to nought. When he stood on his toe, Shuff's eyes peeled back even before he awoke, and he told Henry to fuck off. He came round seconds later, rubbed his face with both hands and said: 'I'm fucken starving, so I am.'

They walked from the train station, passing an orphanage where big-hearted teenagers were decorating, and on into the first half-decent-looking café they saw. They ordered pizzas, Shuff's with extra cheese. He had scanned the menu again after ordering the food, shaken his head and asked the waiter if he served beer. He did. Shuff drank three bottles while Henry had one. Shuff had another pizza and two more beers. Henry had none. The waiter told Shuff that two meals are better than two beatings and laughed. Shuff laughed too, slapping the man on his arm, and Henry worried. They left, overly replenished, bound for the hotel. They found it in Union Square in the centre of the city, an ugly, twelve-storey, newly proud, once poor affair, and checked in. Henry gave Shuff a disposable razor and they went to their rooms. Henry showered and changed and cleaned his teeth. Shuff shat, got stoned and shaved badly. They met in the bar downstairs. Henry thought Shuff's face looked as if it had been shaved with a sharp stick. He looked like he had some kind of disease.

It's 8.23 p.m. and they're standing at the front of the hotel, trams and people and statues in the calm plaza around them. Shuff is smoking a spliff he produced from nowhere and Henry is reading a piece of paper. Henry has a bruise on his cheek, put there by his own hand as it punched him last night. Shuff has said nothing about it. Maybe he doesn't want to.

Henry says: 'If we just jump in a cab we can go straight to this girl's place.'

Shuff draws a deep cloud of tobacco and dope into his lungs and closes his eyes. 'Fucken hell,' he says, blowing out. 'You don't waste any time, do you?'

'What's the point? Let's just do this and see if we can move on.'

'Okay,' says Shuff, sitting down on a low wall and spreading. 'Fuck, it's warm here.'

'Yes,' says Henry. 'Usually is, I heard.'

Shuff nods. 'Tell me the craic, Mr Chancellor. What the fuck are we actually doing again?'

'Okay. Well, the thing is, I want to see if this girl Alina is all right. I've got her address. If she is, then maybe we'll go back to Bucharest and check in with another girl. Just say hi, sort of thing. And then, if you want, we can just go home. To be honest, that's about it. Really I just want to talk to Alina, and then we can play it by ear, sort of thing. It's just a bit of business. I want to make sure she's still working for me.'

Shuff finishes his spliff, smearing it onto the ground with a foot, not having listened to half of what Henry had said. He'd heard the word Thing too many times. It bored him. 'No problem,' he says. 'Are they hookers?'

'No. It's purely business, Shuff. I'm serious about that.'

'Right,' he says, his hope that this trip might turn into some kind of sordid sex vacation beginning to fade. 'The drink's fucken cheap though, eh?'

Henry smiles. He's fine with this. 'Yeah,' he says. 'Let's just get a drink first. Suss the place out.' And then, with a smile: 'No fires though.'

Shuff winks at him and they go.

Alina's city has 334,393 residents, one of whom is what's left of St Parascheva, the Protector of the whole region of Moldavia. She's determined to fulfil that role, her old bones kept at the Metropolitan Cathedral in an enormous silver coffin which the Nazis, the clock against them, found too heavy to nick during the Second World War (Iasians love that nugget of history). Thousands come to pray at St Parascheva's side when they feel the need to be protected, and one of them is Alina, who lives one mile away. She sees her Saint once a month, and she loves her.

Iasi is a city on the rise, slowly emerging from its rigorous past, and often beautiful, dotted with monasteries, churches, botanical gardens, students and, as Western visitors cannot help remarking after a day in its arms, some of the most stunning women on earth. A fourteenth-century child, Iasi has been compared to Rome because of its post on seven hills and because there's often a quiet wind of romance in the warm eastern air.

Much of this, it has been said, is down to the fact that the people carry themselves with a cool Iasian strut and glamour which crushes the often mocking Western eye. It shifts the relevance of the ubiquitous poverty in which most of them grow up, and makes many chat about the discovery of a cool and secret place. Iasian confidence tells the story of a local pride, and it hides the madness of a national shame. Some openly say they're mocked, that they're the butt of a joke which goes around the world, a joke about gypsies and vampires and beggars. Some feel shame too, because they believe they allowed themselves, and the Roma gypsies, an ethnic minority in their own land, to be ground down by Ceausescu before the unifying uprising which most can remember. Behind the doors of that orphanage in Iasi lives and dies the proof of how that man dehydrated so much life in open secrecy and without shame. Many Iasians, many Romanians, have a shame born of the fact that they had made it so far and so well, but that they let one man, whom they trusted to protect them, take everything they had. That shame has surfaced needlessly in too many good hearts across this city and beyond, and it is too often, too unnecessarily, confessed.

Henry Sender likes it. Shuff Sheridan likes it. They love it, sitting in a little bar drinking large beers for pennies, enjoying the calm urbanity through a large window, marvelling at the faces and arses which, they know, form an awesome geographical concentration of divinity. Henry smiles at Shuff as a blonde with a bottom like a heart passes by, confused by the wild adoration in the eyes of the two men. Henry feels how he wanted to feel – calm and perhaps ready to meet Alina. Iasi is making him peaceful, happy to linger on whatever ground he is on. Shuff finishes his beer in his ever-steady hand. He goes back to the bar and returns with a large vodka and two pints. His walk looks unsure.

'You staggering already, Shuff?'

'Nah. Balls hurt after I've had a hard-on. Makes me walk funny.'

'Gosh. That doesn't sound right.'

'Nah. Some wee cunt fucked them up on me. Long story.'

The previous night in London Shuff and his friends had provided the Metropolitan Police with a car chase and denied them a capture. After three bars and a nightclub – during which McFuck had assaulted and robbed a drug dealer in the toilets – they'd walked to Trafalgar Square and talked about nationality, as they often did. They took a vote – they hadn't voted on it together since Shuff left prison – and decided they were British by birth, but with the qualification that they never felt it in Britain. Shuff, as was typical with this matter, changed his mind while pissing in a fountain and said he was Russian instead.

'Me granda was Russian,' he said, shaking his tool in view of all and sundry. 'Communist as fuck.'

They loudly decided a while later, by democratic vote and within earshot of an angry eighteen-strong group of Glasgow Rangers fans, that they were Irish and Celts but with the qualification that they never felt that way in Belfast. Shuff changed his mind and became an Ulsterman, but with the qualification that he was of Russian stock. Blackie agreed with that, but insisted that it be nine-county Ulster and not the six-county Northern Ireland state which forms the majority of Ulster. Shuff disagreed, then agreed, then snorted a whole bag of he didn't know what from the mugged drug dealer, and became entirely Russian again. He lay down in the fountain, holding his breath for two minutes under water, and stood up again announcing he was certain he was Russian and communist as fuck. Gegeen was waiting for him, half bottle of vodka in his hand, to tell him they had all decided they were Nothing. Shuff said that was okay, but that he wanted to be the capital city of Nothing. That was okay with the others. They all agreed that Shuff sometimes behaved like a capital city.

A black Rolls Royce was parked on The Strand, not far away. A uniformed chauffeur sat waiting for his master to return from an hour with a high-class transvestite prostitute, entertaining himself with a CD called *Learn Italian Now*. Sam, who had just been sick, knocked on the passenger-side window of the car. The driver was startled. The door on his side was flung open, and Gegeen and Blackie grabbed him by his collar and wrenched him out and into Shuff's solid body. Shuff head-butted him with precision timing, leaving the man semi-conscious and speaking in what Shuff thought was tongues. It was, in fact, Italian for *I am 59*. Gegeen stole his hat.

Gegeen elected to drive, flooring the car, gasping at its power and laughing at the police horse which bolted when he roared past, the Roller's lights flashing, its occupants ad-libbing songs of old Russia at 62 mph. Police appeared behind them on Regent Street, just as Shuff leaned from the car and punched, at 27 mph, a freerunner who was taking in some of the kerb on his way to Piccadilly Circus, causing the freerunner to bite off half his tongue.

The sights they saw included Oxford Circus, Oxford Street, Marble Arch and Edgware Road, before they came to a complete stop at a Kilburn wall, which airbagged them to their seats. Police arrived as Sam, the last man to get out, was standing up beside his brothers-in-arms, his head feeling like it had just been connected to him. Shuff charged the police car on foot, attempting to ram a fist through the front window as it went into reverse. Inside a man in plain clothes checked a pistol and pointed it at Shuff as he stood still, then grew smaller as the car moved backwards. It stopped and Shuff was joined by his comrades in a defensive line. Two other sirens whined in the air. McFuck had slipped out, carjacked a hairdresser, and called out to the gang. Before Shuff climbed aboard, he picked up twenty-one-year-old Stevie Doherty from County Wexford, who was passing by, by the balls and neck and marched with him towards the waiting police car. He held Stevie up like a shield as a gun was trained on him from behind an open car door. He walked closer and closer before hurling Stevie into the air, onto the bonnet of the vehicle. By the time the police had ducked and popped back up to check on their quarry, Shuff was in McFuck's new car and they were speeding off down Victoria Road. That's Stevie Doherty's favourite story.

They ended up in a shebeen in Neasden known to a friend of Blackie's and Sam's, and drank solidly for another hour and a half. A fight ensued between Sam and a Belfast socialist called Drew at the bar. After Drew was punched by Gegeen and robbed by McFuck, he was barred for life (it was easier than barring Gegeen and McFuck). Shuff didn't even notice the fight. He was too busy attempting to vaginally fist a wart-ridden, middle-aged ex-prostitute in a dark corner. The corner was dark only because he had punched the light out. It was, they all agreed, a good night. Shuff had made it to his hotel at 5.41 a.m. Henry was waiting in the lobby, looking like he was having some kind of panic attack.

Shuff had told the whole story to Henry on the plane, explaining with a straight face that a vodka-soaked hand does not provide enough lubrication to easily conduct such an intense sexual act. Henry was beside himself with laughter, thriving on the way Shuff casually explained the details while trying simultaneously to read an article about Romanian sheep's cheese in the in-flight magazine. Henry laughed because he knew it was true and because he wasn't there. He hadn't broken any rules and felt no shame or guilt, and the story somehow began to hide the memory of that wedding ring being ripped from that newly married barman's finger. Shuff hadn't even got out of his seat on the plane, he hadn't even phoned anyone or smoked or shouted anything, and Henry felt they were learning from each other. He thought he understood what that Last Door was, and believed he could see it. He was certain he couldn't pass through it, but he now knew it was there. He knew Shuff had gone somewhere extreme in his mind and wasn't coming back. Understanding this gave him a kind of certain pleasure, a sense that he at least comprehended the absence of parameters in the mind of a man well beyond his power. He didn't even worry or say a word when Shuff later lifted someone else's bag from the carousel at Otopeni Airport in Bucharest, searched it in the taxi and took from it a Diesel denim shirt, which he is now wearing. Shuff left his own bag, which contained a towel and a pear, behind.

Shuff told Henry, after Henry had asked him high above France, that he had been Saved after hearing the Reverend Ian Paisley speak in Belfast ten years ago. It was a purely religious thing for Shuff, his hazy personal politics being somewhere between communist, fascist, hedonist, sexist and Belfast. What had struck Shuff was that Paisley had bellowed the word Jezebel to the scantily clad and married secretary Shuff was with, without so much as a breath of concern that Shuff might kill him. Shuff listened on, believing that the man had something to say, and that he had the guts to say it. As was usual, he had been looking everywhere for answers at the time, and Paisley with his Lamb's Blood, his solid shields of belief, his guarantee of the afterlife, seemed to have them. On a whim, Shuff was baptised and Born Again. Two years later he was out, convinced that most of those Born Again don't really believe what they say they do, seeing the thing as a submissive way to live and die. He took with him five other recent, disreputable recruits who had also been looking for answers. Those six souls, now all destined to burn, spent the following two weeks fantastically off their heads in a caravan park in County Derry. It had been a creative fortnight, during which Shuff, and the other five, had read a book called *The Last Door*, which he'd found in one of the caravans, and then burned down a local church. They don't remember how many, or whose, caravans they used, how many they ultimately decided to torch, only that they all took something meaningful from the book.

Towards the end of their holiday, they had fallen in with some men who invited them to an illegal dogfight. During the fight, the fearsome six had fallen out with the organisers, and a fight more brutal than that in the pit ensued. Shuff broke a head and left with a champion pit bull under his arm. He had arrived back in Belfast some days later with thousands of bold blue letters on his body, and had drunk vodka after vodka as his hungry hound licked the inky, congealing blood from his freshly needled skin. A month later he had made it onto the front cover of *Tattoo Monthly*, and the police had kept a copy.

He said they had worked out their own way of going about things. The guys came up with what they wanted done, and picked another one of the gang to do it. It kept them all, they suspected, abnormally strong, fully committed to the high nothings of the gang. Shuff had known he was a true believer when Gegeen asked him to hand himself in for smashing up a circus float during a festival. Shuff had been hallucinating on acid at the time and had believed the clowns were some kind of piss-take of his heavily made-up wife, for reasons no one ever admitted to understanding. Shuff duly handed himself in, was given a reasonable three-month suspended sentence, developed a whimsical interest in going to jail, punched a prison officer and a policeman, dragged the judge across his bench, carted him into his own quarters and beat him unconscious while holding his foot against the door. By the time the police grabbed Shuff, beat him, Maced him, beat him, doubled their number, subdued him and rearrested him, the judge had lost three pints of blood and the memory of the first thirty-one years of his life.

Shuff was given eleven years and served just four. He'd been an excellent, contented prisoner who secured unmonitored family visits, and a small drug-dealing business, towards the end of his stay. He got out on licence a year ago, knowing he was one serious member of one serious gang. He didn't know that the others had already left Northern Ireland on the advice of seventeen men with angry guns. Shuff had raged for a month. After he calmed down, he made a plan and, over two weeks, managed to kick the living shit out of eleven of the seventeen men. He was arrested three times for these crimes, but — as was always the case — no one would ever say that Shuff, living on licence or not, had anything to do with any crime. As was so often the case, there was scant evidence on which to hang the conviction of Shuff Sheridan. Indeed, cautious rumour had it that he once nailed a woman, a secretary, to a wooden floor for mentioning his name in an inappropriate place.

11.51 p.m. Henry and Shuff are in a nightclub with garish lights, loud electronic music and lots of locals who know it's the dodgiest joint in town. It's the sort of Euro music, Henry thinks, which holds back the countries in which it is loved. They'd had a few more than Henry would have liked in the previous bar, and one or two others in a bar close by. Henry feels ragged drunk, his speech slurred and his brain all spongy. He's kind of written off doing anything businesslike tonight. It's late and, besides, Shuff's on a party roll and Henry's not really going to be able to stand in his way. Alina's disappearance can wait until the morning.

They'd passed an extraordinary queue on the street outside. Extraordinary because of its sudden beauty, because the girls whispered openly into each others' delicate ears, their big, wide, dark eyes rolling over the English-speaking pair after Shuff had seized and kissed a stray, graceful hand he found in front of him and said *Mamma Mia*. Henry, using all the force of his life, would not have been able to stop Shuff joining the queue – from the front. He had shrugged. Yes, he was drunk. Yes, he could have had another drink, but he was a little edgy again. He preferred it when Shuff appeared to be more in control than he was now. He thought to himself that some of the guys looked like the sort of people who might stab him. He felt they'd walked into a bad part of town and that Shuff's eyeing of every woman in the club might be a red rag to a lot of bulls. Henry just didn't know, but again, there's nothing you can do with Shuff that Shuff doesn't want to do. Besides, Henry always feels as if he's going to be stabbed, and always that he's in a bad part of town. They had stepped into a short corridor and into the club.

There are lots of seats in here, once-plush soft semi-circles bracketing small, round tables. It isn't possible to tell what colour these seats are, beyond dark. Henry lets Shuff get to the bar first so he can pick the largest vacant space in the seating area and wave Shuff over with a smile, away from the stabbers and their girlfriends. Henry tries now to keep his eyes to himself, taking out the mobile phone which never rings and pretending someone has sent him a text message. The network is called ZAPP. He laughs falsely at the screen and presses a button or two. He sits a foot further round to the right, a foot further away from the bar, where there's more spring in the cushion. The seat might be purple. It's hard to tell with the flashing, whirling, out-of-sync, multicolour, seventies-style lighting system.

At the bar, Henry sees that Shuff has a heavy arm around the shoulder of a man of equal size. He's shouting something in broad Belfast into the man's ear.

'Me granda was Russian — communist as fuck.' The man is nodding, smiling and trying to get away. Please let him go, Shuff.

Shuff returns with two pintish jugs of beer and a glass of water. It's not a glass of water. It just looks so clear and fresh that it appears to be a glass of water. It's six vodkas. He sits down with a heavy drop and folds up his denim sleeves. VIDERANDDENIERPRO.

'I could get used to this shite,' his voice raised, a hand wrapping around the glass. He pours it into his body, head all the way back. The glass is empty. He spreads his legs and belches loudly. 'Some fucken talent in here, eh?'

Henry takes a sip of beer.

'Yes. I'm half pissed.'

'Aye, me too. Still drunk from last night, so I am.'

'Yes.'

'Can you get any drugs round here, d'you reckon? Anything hard?'

'No. They're very strict about that.' Henry doesn't know. He just doesn't want Shuff to start hunting.

'I'm talking about the drugs, not the rules. Chill out,

Henry, fuck's sake.'

'Sorry. I'm a bit woozy. The lights are a bit too much.'

'The lights? You take fits or something?'

'No. I'm fine. Let's have these and go.'

'The back of me arse. Grand fucken spot this. I want me hole.'

Oh God.

And then: 'I'd say this place is full of wee hooers. Those girls you know from here are all dirty wee things, eh?'

'No. I told you that. They don't meet people. It's just an internet thing.'

Shuff laughs, taking out his spliff paraphernalia.

'Aye, but they show off their holes and all for money, isn't that right?'

'Sort of.'

'Well, there you are. Not a million miles wrong now, am I?'

'Not a million miles.'

Shuff licks the paper and rolls up his spliff, his eyes scanning the joint as he goes. He spots two men talking on the half-empty floor as they look at him. So does Henry. Henry looks away. Shuff gets up, lights up and walks towards them, a thick, colour-morphing trail of smoke dragging behind him. Henry wonders what he's doing here. He takes out his phone again and this time sends a text message. To himself. It reads *fuck this fuck this*. A moment later and it arrives. Henry reads it and nods in full agreement.

The men stop talking as Shuff approaches. They're early twenties, well-dressed, wearing cheap jeans which they hide the labels of, on the prowl for a good night out. Shuff holds the spliff out to see if there's any takers. One man looks around him briefly, then takes it. He inhales deeply, coughing as it goes down.

'Good fucken stuff, so it is. Best in Belfast.' The man nods, tears welling in his eyes. The other gives a negative nod when he's offered the smoke.

'Fair enough,' says Shuff. 'You fellas have any coke or Es or anything like that?'

'Hmmm?'

'Cocaine? Ecstasy? Any drugs, like?'

'No. Where from?' Music racketing.

'Belfast. You local?'

'Hmmm?'

'Are you local? Lo-cal? From here?' Shuff points at the ground. He looks quickly back at Henry.

'Iasi?'

'Aye. Yash.'

'Yes. Iasi.'

'Dead on. If you know anyone with any drugs, find me. I've plenty of money, so I have. I wouldn't mind me hole either, to be honest. Hole? You know hole?' He points at his testicles.

'Hmmm?'

'Aye, well. Don't fucken stare at me big lad, unless you've got something to say for yourself. That goes for you too, you no-tongued fucker. Right?'

'Hmmm?'

'Aye.' A dismissive wave of a hand. 'Good luck.'

He returns to Henry's side, sits and spreads. 'What's the standard of English like around here?'

'I don't know. So-so, I think.'

'So fuck all.'

'Why did you lot throw money and all onto that fire in the pub?'

'What?'

'Why did you throw money and stuff onto that fire?'

'I don't know. No reason.'

'Have you got a lot of money?'

'No. Well, when I need it I get it. You know the craic, Hen.'

'You were keen on this job, on the money.'

'Oh aye. This is easy money. I take it when it comes along. I wanted to go too. To Romania. Granda was Russian, so he was.'

'Communist as fuck?'

'Aye.'

'Yes.'

'I don't know what part he was from. He fucked me granny down the docks and fucked off.'

'Oh, so you never knew him?' Henry considers that Shuff's grandmother may have been a prostitute, but he won't say it.

Shuff shakes his head, eyes collecting all around. 'Nah, fuck. Never. He might have been from here for all I know.'

'This isn't Russia.'

'Is it not? Well, USSR. Soviet.'

'Was he USSR or actually Russian?'

'Henry. Read my lips. Fuck knows.'

'How do you know he was communist as fuck?'

'Me granny said he had one of them hammers tattooed on his arm.'

'The hammer and sickle?'

'Aye.'

'Yes.'

'I always thought of him as some big fuck-off Russian sailor. Ivan the Terrible, you know? But a pirate. Blowing the fuck out of everything in the water. That's what I used to think years ago.'

'Yes.'

'Your round.'

'Yes. What you having?'

'A pint of that shite and a sextuple vodka.'

'A sextuple?'

'Aye.' A pause. 'What?'

'Bloody hell. You'll be on your arse.'

A pause. 'Don't tell me how to drink, Hen.'

'Okay. You're the boss.'

'Aye.' Shuff nods. 'At least one of us is.'

Henry gets the drinks and a shake of a head from the woman at the bar and turns around. Shuff is disappearing into the crowd, the two guys he spoke with leading the way. His stomach jumps. The drinks spill a little on his hands. He sits down, wipes his hands on his jeans and thinks he'll spread his legs and look around. Shuff has now vanished into the thickening crowd.

Two long, slim girls come over and point at the space in the semi-circle and say something in Romanian. Henry smiles and nods them in. He looks away, into the lights, as they sit down and straighten their skirts. Their legs shine. Henry is nervous. A tall man with a goatee beard walks over and sits beside one of the girls, right where Shuff had been sitting. He talks and waves his hands around, ignoring the Englishman. The girls pout and say nothing. Henry thinks of his phone.

Shuff is led out of the entrance to the club, into the corridor and through another door. It closes behind him. There's music playing and half a dozen guys are smoking pot and chatting.

'Well, what about yiz?' he says.

One of the two men speaks to a man, and the man eyes Shuff.

'Hey,' he says, standing up, tall and classy. 'I'm Bran.'

'Bran? Jesus. Shuff.'

'Hi, Shuff.' The men shake hands. Everyone is looking at Shuff, at his tattoos. 'So, you want coca?'

'Aye. What you got?'

'How much?'

'What you got?'

'How much you got? The money?'

'Show me the coca first, big lad.'
'What?'
'Show me the coca first, big lad.'

A man says something loud and fast in Romanian to Bran. Bran nods.

Shuff smiles: 'Listen to me, Bran. Don't fucken take the piss.' He points at the guy who had called to Bran. 'You neither. Talk in English, get me the coca or go and fuck yourselves up your Romanian fucken arses. Right?'

Bran looks confused. Shuff takes a step closer. Everyone tenses. Bran smiles.

'It's okay,' he says. He reaches over to the man who had called him, and a small package is passed between them. He holds it out. 'You like this?'

Shuff takes it from his hand, scowling around. Two girls enter the room quietly. They sit down on one tatty chair. One of them lights a cigarette. Shuff eyes her firm, open cleavage and she watches him. He winks at her. 'All right, wee love?' The men look at each other.

Shuff dips a finger into the bag and runs it over his gums. He looks again at the men. They await his verdict. He thinks it's fine, but pauses – dramatic effect. He holds the bag up to the light, brings it back down and takes another wet finger-load. He wipes it along his top gum again, looking around, smacking his lips. Bran begins to frown. Shuff smiles. Bran smiles. The others smile. Shuff nods.

'How much do you want for it?'

Bran looks at his friend, who says something in Romanian. Shuff looks at the friend.

'Speak English, big lad.'

They all look at each other again.

'Where from?' says Bran.

'Belfast.'

'In Ireland?'

'Aye.'

Bran smiles, knowingly. 'Hey, Podge and Rodge?'

'Wha?'

'The TV.' A pause. 'Puppets. Podge and Rodge.'

'Right.' A pause. 'How much do you want for this? There's not much of it.'

'It's okay,' says Bran, a bigger smile. 'You party, Shuff.'

Shuff nods. He takes out his wallet and one of many £50 notes among a fortune in Romanian lei. Bran watches. Shuff looks at Bran as he rolls the note into a tube. He approaches the smoking girl. 'You got a mirror, love?'

She looks to Bran. Bran looks to Shuff, not knowing what to say. He looks to the girl. 'Me-roar,' he says.

A man behind quietly says *oglinda* – mirror in Romanian. The girl takes a little mirror from her bag and hands it to Shuff. He looks in it and strokes a tuft of his self-cut hair. They all stare. He bends down, putting the mirror on the girl's fine, half-naked thigh. He pours out all the cocaine and makes it into a thick line with his little finger.

'Nice and fine,' he says, looking up at Bran, and then to the girl. 'She's ready to go.'

The girl – Elena – doesn't know if she should continue to smoke. Her cigarette continues to burn. Shuff snorts all the cocaine into one nostril in one go. He breathes out big, blowing the girl's smoke away from her face, causing her to blink and jerk back.

'Not three fucken bad,' he says, catching the mirror before it falls, fingers on her leg. He gives it to her. He stands up and hands the empty bag back to Bran.

'Bran,' he says, and laughs. 'Some fucken name you have there, big lad. Do you shite yourself much?'

Bran smiles. They all laugh nervously. Shuff looks again at

the smoking girl and offers another wink. He steps to the side and leans against a sink, ready to skin up a spliff. 'So, what's the craic round here then?'

One of the men leaves the room without a word, nodding only to Shuff as he goes. Shuff nods back. 'All right, big lad.'

Goatee turns to Henry, leaning across the seat, as he ends a fake phone call.

'Hey. You English?' He looks stern.

'Yes. Well, I speak English. Yes.' What the fuck.

'Cool. Me too. What you do in Iasi?' The girls stare at him, silent and glorious, shining. Henry folds his arms.

'Just visiting. With a friend.'

'You like the girls, yes?'

'No, no, not at all. Well, yes, they're very pretty.'

'I understand.' The man looks away and says something to the girls. They laugh out loud. Henry smiles and hugs himself. Goatee waves a mustachioed man over. He tells him something, quietly into his ear. The man laughs and looks at Henry. Henry is dying, eyes not focusing properly. Where the fuck is Shuff? Every word's a slur. He'll slur more now he's thought of it. His foot starts to bounce. His phone doesn't ring.

A broad, bony-faced, Shuff-sized man enters the side room and spies the foreigner. A firm hand.

'Hey. You the Irish man?'

'Aye.' Shuff returns a firm hand. 'Shuff.'

'Shuff. Cool. I'm Yan.'

'Dead on. You from here?'

'Yes. I live in Iasi, mate. But I'm from Russia.'

'Russia? Dead on. Me granda was Russian.'

'Hey, really?'

'Aye. Communist as fuck.'

'I'm not communist, mate. I'm capitalist.'
'Aye, well.'
'Hey, what you here for, mate?'
'Doing a wee job just.'
'Cool. Where you stay?'
'Fuck knows. Some hotel in the centre.'
'Cool. You here on business then, yes?'
'Aye.'
'What kind of business?'
'This and that. What do you do?'
'This and that. Hey, you want to do business?'

Shuff smiles. He's sussing this man out. What does he want to hear about? 'What do you want, big lad?' says Shuff, looking into the man's eyes. 'You're not going to fuck me about, lemme tell you.'

'No. I don't want to.' A pause. 'Hey, you like this girl?' He points at Elena, the smoker. She's twenty and looks like Demi Moore did, only more so.

Shuff winks at her. 'Aye, very nice.'

'Cool.' The Russian calls to her and she looks disgusted. She stands up, walks to the back of the room and lifts a bottle of beer from a sideboard. 'Shuff. Go with her.' Then, lower: 'You can fuck.'

Shuff looks into the man's eyes again, as if stamping some kind of firm message into his memory. He draws away and looks at all the people in the room. He's no longer the centre of attention.

'One second,' says Shuff. He turns and yanks open the door. Two men are standing outside. They jump. 'All right, lads?' Shuff pushes through, considering briefly that some fucken eejit might have put them there to keep him closed in, but he has other things on his mind. He walks up the corridor and puts his head into the club. He can see Henry sitting beside

Goatee, talking, arms folded. He turns around, pushes past the two, goes back into the room and closes the door. 'Aye. No bother.'

Yan smiles. 'What's wrong?'

'Not one fucken thing. Listen, mate.' Shuff steps up to his face. 'If anything funny happens to me, this is what I'll do.'

Yan shakes his head. 'Hey, what do you mean?'

'This is what I'll do, right? I'll rip your fucken spine out. You hear me? You got that, Yan?' A pause. Yan tries to smile. 'You understand what I'm saying?'

Yan looks around. There's a lump in his throat that he hasn't felt in years and years. 'Hey, there's no problem. I want to be friendly, Shuff. No fucking problem.'

Shuff turns to face the girl. She's at a door at the other side of the room, washing beer around in her mouth. Shuff gives Yan one last stony look and walks through the room, knocking a stray leg out of the way. 'All right, love?' Another wink at the shining Elena as she pushes open the door, beer in hand. Shuff follows, eyes dropping to her ravishing rear end.

Goatee now sits on one side of Henry. The other man, who looks like Goatee but with only a moustache, sits to his other side. They talk to Henry in English, then occasionally across him in Romanian. These are among the worst moments of his life. They're what he imagined in his most terrifying thoughts. Death must be easier. His foot bounces like it's on fire. His heart bangs like it's demanding to get out.

Goatee speaks. 'Hey. You want to fuck?'

'Sorry?'

'Fuck? We like fuck.'

'Fuck? No. I'm waiting for my friend.'

'It's cool.' A pause. 'You like gay?'

'Gay?'

'Gay fuck?'

'No. Sorry.'

The other man shakes his head at Goatee. He speaks first softly, then loudly. It sounds like a string of insults. Henry stares straight ahead, a red light beats on and off into his eyes. A man comes into view on the dance floor, openly pointing at him, calling someone to his side.

Goatee cuts in over his friend: 'You like think we stupid Romania fucks?'

'No.' Henry sounds sarcastic. Just two letters, yet slurred. 'I mean, no. Look, I'm going to go, okay?'

'No,' says Goatee. 'You fucking say why no gay fuck.'

'Look, I have to meet my friend.'

Goatee's friend slaps Henry, not hard, on his face. Henry burns all over. Both feet bounce. He keeps staring straight ahead, arms folded tight. The two men in front walk over. One of them is the guy Shuff had gripped in friendship at the bar. He's the one who rockets his face into Henry's.

'Hey, you fuck,' he shouts. 'You fucking gay fuck. You fuck gay. You fat-face friend fucking gay.'

Goatee and his friend pull back, scared.

'Look,' says Henry, voice all high. 'Look.' The man grabs his neck, pushing him back against the seat, pushing back the lump in his throat. Henry puts two flat palms up and grunts.

Goatee joins in: 'You fucking gay England fuck.'

Shuff's short, stout penis is as deep as it can be in Elena's throat. A spliff burns an inch from his lips. He moans through his nose, noise and smoke pouring out. He starts riding her face, feeling her tight tongue flicking his glans. She lets her teeth gripstroke as he pumps. He fucks harder. Spits out the spliff. It hits off the back wall, flashing in the little dark room. He grabs the sides of her head, taking control, ramming her

into him and pushing her out, fast as a jackhammer. Ecstasy.
 'Ohhhhh you fucken, Jesus, you fucken bitch, yes, yes, yes, yes.' His hands are all over her head. A little finger slips into her ear and starts to move in and out.

The man with his hand on Henry – Cezar – spits into his face. Henry can't even pull back. He closes his eyes. He sees Alina holding a pan.
 'You fucking England.' The man shakes his gripped hand, Henry's dizzy head spins more with the force. His heart is steady, but as fast as it can be without failing.
 'Sorry,' he squeaks.
 'England bastard man.' Cezar's hand pulls back. It punches Henry. He sees Gegeen stripping the skin from the robbed barman's ring. He sees his dying ex–foster mother, bright and smiling. He wants to run forever. He could find somewhere to hide. There was a disused signal house at the train station. Goatee pulls out a knife, a six-inch blade.

Shuff's about to blow. The girl sinks her teeth in hard. Way too hard. There's a crack on the back of his head. He's not sure for a second. Then he's sure. He's been hit. The back of his head fizzes. His temper explodes. She bites harder. Shuff rams his thumbs into her eyes. They shoot an inch back into her head, rupturing tissue. Her mouth springs open. She falls back, a gargling scream. Semen shoots across her face. Shuff spins around. It's Bran with a block of wood. The Russian's behind Bran. More semen spurts. The side of Shuff's fist crashes into the wood. It flies back. Bran's balance is lost. He takes a quick step back. Yan, the Russian, has a gun. It's on its way up. Shuff throws himself and sends Yan crashing backwards. Shuff grips his head and rams it into the wall. The block of wood hits him again. He twists Yan's wrist, hard, fast.

It breaks. Another scream. Yan's gun hits the ground. The wood again. Shuff grabs the revolver. He turns around and fires at Bran. He's cool about killing him. The chamber turns, but no bullet. Bran steps back, out of the open door. Shuff piles through after him, pulling at his trousers, dick swinging, semi-hard. Bran runs through the room calling. The far door opens. It's the two guards. And three men in the room already. They all brace themselves. Shuff stops. Yan runs out from behind. Six men. Shuff shrugs. He finishes pulling up his trousers. He smiles as he thinks how he always leaves his lovers right after the act, how he's always gone before the cum cools.

He laughs a little now as he tucks his aching penis into his pants. There's blood mixed in with the semen. He does up a button. He zips. He smiles more. Six men. Yan is one of them. That fucking Russian. Shuff drops the smile and stares at him, and he stares back. Shuff looks into the chamber of the weapon. There are two bullets, unaligned. Six men.

'Great blowjob,' he says, bringing the revolver to his side. 'Romanian girls are real fucken sluts, eh?'

Another man enters the room and quietly closes the door. He pulls a gun from his belt. He points it at Shuff. Shuff ignores it. It's what works for him. Seven men, one woman. Yan speaks. He talks to them all and points at his broken wrist, his twisted hand. They all nod. Bran says something back to him. Shuff thinks of Henry. Holy fuck. What about Henry? They must know they're together. Maybe they've got him.

He lifts his hand again, forgetting if he's lined up a bullet in the chamber, and re-checks. The gun pointing at him is shaking, irrelevant. Shuff turns around. Elena is feeling her way out behind him, squinting, weeping. He puts the revolver into her face. He grabs her head, pulls her to him and puts the gun into her mouth. He straightens his arm and arcs her around him in a semi-circle, as if pulling her by a fish hook. He stops when her back is to the men. Shuff's facing them. She's facing him. Her mouth is wide. Half of the chamber of the gun is in there now. He pushes and she starts walking backwards, tears falling from her closed, bleeding eyes. The Russian shakes his head.

'You no fucking leave, Shuff.'

Shuff nods and smiles. 'You wanna fucken bet?'

Yan looks at the man with the gun. More words. The man nods. Shuff pulls Elena around further. The gun's now pointing straight at Yan, through her. Again: 'You wanna fucken bet, Yan the Man? Answer me, big lad.'

The Russian considers his predicament. He says something to his friend at the door with the gun. Shuff pulls the gun downwards. The girl dips, bending her legs. She doesn't know if she's blind. Her head aches like it's being stabbed. She's pushed backwards. The Russian straightens himself near the wall. The back of her head is walked gently towards his crotch.

'You wanna fucken bet with Shuff? You wanna fucken bet with me, Yanski?'

Yan speaks again. His tones are calm, his palms up. The girl wheezes. She can breathe only through her nose, blood bubbling. The man at the door puts his gun away.

'No,' says Shuff, hand out, fingers waggling. 'Give it to me.' The man takes it out again, raging inside. Yan shakes his head.

'No gun. You fucking go now.'

'Were you trying to rob me or what?'

'You go, Shuff.' The man puts his gun away again. Shuff thinks of Henry. He checks his wallet's there. His passport's in it. It's there. He stares at Yan. Yan stares. Lips curl. Yan looks away.

Says Shuff: 'If you won't donate the gun, you're donating

the slut.'

He lifts the gun up and Elena carefully rises with it, terrified, face like an operation. He walks her backwards to the door. His balls throb – always do after ejaculation. He fixes them with a hand. He stares at Yan. Yan looks away again. No one wants to play the staring game, the animal game. He reaches for the handle, opens the door, pushes her out and closes it behind them. He spits on his free hand and runs it through his hair. Elena makes some kind of involuntary sound.

'I know,' says Shuff.

Henry's pinned to a wall. Three men surround him. One, Goatee, breaks off and returns to the table, knife in his hand. He picks up Shuff's pint and sits down, toying with the blade.

Consternation grips as bleeding Elena is walked in. People make way. Shuff walks her slowly towards the unfolding violence in the corner. Music pumping.

'Wait here, love,' he says. He pushes the gun further into her mouth. Her jaw aches. It's in up to the trigger casing, lodged hard. Her nostrils flare. She thinks she might choke and die. Shuff leaves her. She holds her hands out, feeling around, but no one comes close. She stands frozen, steel deep in her face, too scared to touch the gun in case it explodes, awaiting her fate to an electronic beat.

Shuff walks to Goatee. Goatee looks up, drunk. Shuff reaches down and locks a hand onto his throat. He pulls him from his seat and throws him onto the floor, knife flailing, unguided with the shock. Shuff picks up the round table and tilts it. The glasses all crash down onto Goatee. He screams and slams the knife into a falling ashtray. Shuff turns the table upside down. He grabs its central leg with both hands. He lifts it high, his legs parted, and rams it down onto Goatee's face. Glass shatters, shards scattering across the floor, 360 degrees. The knife hits the floor. The two men holding Henry look round. Henry's bleeding. Shuff drops the table and it rolls behind him. An artery has severed in Goatee's neck. The two men take their hands off Henry. Shuff steps forward and puts a hand on Henry's shoulder.

"Mon, big lad,' he says – and Henry is protected. He steps out, jelly-legged, to Shuff's side. He shivers. He's saved.

'Take their fucking money, Shuff,' he says, spitting. Shuff puts out a hand. Henry can see blood on it.

'Money,' he says.

'This shit,' says Cezar.

Shuff steps forward and the man flattens himself against the wall, regretting his words.

'I won't ask you again, big lad,' says Shuff.

The man reaches behind. He takes out his wallet and gives it to Shuff. Shuff hands it to Henry. The other man is slower, more terrified. He gives it over.

'C'mon to fuck,' says Shuff.

Henry spits onto Goatee's face as he passes. A pond of blood is spreading across the floor. Henry sees Elena, alone, lost where she stands, wood-finished metal handle sticking out of her mouth, lights flashing into her blind face. It's horrible. Shuff reaches out and grips the handle. It's coated with saliva. He tugs and pushes, taking her again on an unseen mission, twisting her back to the door and starting to walk her. Henry will not comment. It's surreal. Just surreal. The club clears a path as the two men and the girl walk through, bad music still bouncing around. Shuff recognises none of the men on the way through. Elena might have died if he did. He pushes her out into the corridor and to the exit. A shirt-and-tied bouncer stands dead still, smiling, nodding, scared. On the street, Henry feels a light breeze. He looks all around. No one's coming to get him.

Shuff nods to the bouncer: 'Tell Yan to watch out for me.'

The bouncer nods. Shuff yanks the weapon from Elena's mouth, teeth tearing from her gums. She screams from deep in her throat. Two teeth hit the ground.

'Jesus!' Henry shouts. 'Okay, Shuff, that's enough.'

Shuff looks at him, wiping the gun on his shirt, motioning it towards Elena. 'You don't know what this cunt did to me.'

'Jesus,' says Henry. He's dizzy. He looks at the teeth on the ground. Another abseils from her mouth on a string of blood. She can't remember where she is.

Shuff nods to the bouncer. 'Get her a glass of water.'

The bouncer nods and goes inside. People in the corridor pretend not to look. Shuff and Henry wait. Henry wants to bounce his foot, to jump, to shake himself. He doesn't want to say anything else. He's done. He's got no more useless orders. He hopes no one walks into the street. Elena cuts what you'd call a tragic figure. There's nothing he can do.

Shuff radars around, gun at his side, bullet lined up, a wild, guided missile. Elena has his mobile phone in her bag inside the club. She remembers that much now. She sneaked it out of his back pocket while he was in the throes of passion. Now she figures if this man finds out, he'll probably kill her.

The bouncer returns, handing a tall glass to Elena, but she doesn't even know. Shuff takes it from him and puts it into Elena's hand.

'Drink it,' he says. 'Wash yer mouth out.'

Elena slowly lifts it to her battered face, resting it on a bottom lip that burns like a fire.

Says Shuff, to the bouncer: 'You make sure that Russian cunt gets the message, right?'

The bouncer nods. He smiles. Shuff winks. He takes a full grip around one side of the pistol and looks at it. They all look at it. He rams it, a fast uppercut, a sudden flash, into

Elena's face. It hits the bottom of the glass. There's a crack as it crumples into her, shattering, shards driven inwards. She makes a sound from somewhere and falls back, collapsing onto the ground, smacking her head, her beauty in ribbons. The bouncer steps away, horrified, terrified.

'Make sure you tell him,' reminds Shuff.

Inside, Goatee gives the last kicks of his life. He's lost too much blood. The ambulance will take too long. He's going to die.

Henry creases forward in some kind of pain. He's shaking, immobile. He feels Shuff's hand on his shoulder, lifting him up.

'You're all right, big lad. You don't know what she did to me in there. You'd have done the same thing.' Henry wouldn't have. Nothing like it.

The bouncer hopes they'll both go away forever. Elena lies still, spitting gently, sharp pieces of glass buried into her tongue, the roof of her mouth and up her nose, blinded and scarred and damaged forever. Shuff leads Henry slowly away. They walk for a while, cool night-time breeze, directionless, turning random corners, Shuff's eyes covering everything. He tucks the gun into his waist. He's sure no one else is going to fuck with him.

Henry stops. 'I have to go to Alina's. I can't take this.'

Shuff nods. 'Just a bad situation, big lad. That shit happens every day. Don't sweat it.'

'I'm going,' says Henry.

'Not without me,' says Shuff.

'I can't cope with you.'

'Wise up, fuck's sake. You'd have been fucken raped in there or something. Think of it that way.'

'I can't do this, Shuff.'

'Hen. Alina probably works for guys like that. They're

probably fucken sitting there now. You can't go without me, big lad. That's my job.' Shuff rubs the back of his head. Blood is hardening in the hair. It annoys him.

Henry's lost. He wipes blood from his face and thinks of that girl, Elena, cut to bits on her own street by a madman from Belfast. 'Jesus Christ,' he says. He might cry.

'Think about it,' says Shuff. 'I'm only doing what you wanted me to do.'

'Jesus Christ.' His voice rises. 'I didn't want you to ruin a girl's fucking life.'

Shuff shakes his head, pissed off with Henry's attitude. 'You wanna go without me?' he asks. 'Then just fucken go.'

Henry's eyes drop to the ground. He thinks. He knows he can't. He really can't. He just hasn't got the strength. He knows himself too well. The situation would have been a lot worse if there'd been no Shuff, no Protector. Where would he be now without him? 'No. Come on.'

'All right, big lad,' says Shuff. 'One drink, then we'll go. Me fucken balls are killing me.'

'No. We're going now.'

'Ten minutes. There's a bar down that street. I didn't even get to drink that fucken pint.'

'FOR FUCK'S SAKE.'

Shuff shakes his head. 'Ten minutes, Hen. I won't say it again.'

'Ten minutes. No more. I can't take any more.'

Henry's going to have his first-ever large, neat vodka. There's hardly any money in his assailants' wallets, but it buys the round.

12

Alina had been christened Elena, after the glamorous wife of Romanian dictator Nicolae Ceausescu. Elena Petrescu cast a spell over the devout Stalinist communist she married in 1939, and later a spell over her native land. She was a chemist of world renown, a beauty with brains at the side of her man, complementing his charisma and emboldening the emotive nationalism which saw him, fearlessly, patriotically, challenge Moscow's policy of the ultra-centralisation of the USSR throughout his reign. She rose from no one to icon, to soar beside him as he reached out for and took charge of a proud people, lifting them from the hole of their ravaged history. He became General Secretary of the Romanian Communist Party, President and Head of State, and she was always there, with proud heart and flawless features. When he appointed her Deputy President, she accepted because that was what the people wanted. She had to accept, for the sake of her nation. No woman has ever taken Elena's place. It was this woman who fired the imagination of male and female across the land, and it's this woman today who lives on in the names of a million Romanians, all christened by proud parents who loved all the daughters of their country. The name Elena means Sunlight.

That was, at least, the story. But Elena was no chemist. Her qualifications were retrospectively arranged by her husband, her schooling having been limited and her studies a failure. And she was no great force for the nation, backing Nicolae to the hilt when he planned to turn the Roma into gypsy slaves, when he flirted with the idea of genetic engineering and a chilling Hitlerite programme that would have created what he liked to call the Robot Work Force. Her hand was in his when he tore a bold, earned economy down in the seventies, and she ate well with him when he sold the nation's honest achievements to foreigners in the eighties, causing his own people – with Moscow's cold consent – to hunger for food, and ail and die for medicine. And there she was at the end, shot to death at his side after a trial during which she raged that she would never claim the insanity which could have spared her life. In unison, the couple even managed to sing the opening words of the Russian version of 'The Internationale' before the bullets sealed their fate. Their own lawyer, Nicu Teodorescu, called the Ceausescus' reign *a monster with two heads*. He said their execution was *the most beautiful Christmas in my whole life*. Nicolae and Elena, the Romanian patriots, had the murders of 60,000 on their conscience, but you would never have known it.

Yet it's true that no one has ever replaced Elena. Her name still inspires a perverse sense of awe in barren fields, echoing factories, at her busy graveside and near orphanages where scarred children live – innocent children, abused to death. A million Elenas make a people smile, maybe in the hope that one of them will come to the rescue of a myth that so many loved so much during the testing years of so little, the eighties years which the dictator christened The Era of Light. But Elena herself may have damaged the image of women more than anyone. It is a society still controlled by men, with some of the same old generalising generals still lurking around the levers of power, and many of them like to believe that their beautiful women are Elenas, icons of femininity, of a revised Romanian grace.

Alina hated Elena, the name, the woman, and the lies which fooled and robbed her land for an unbreakable ego the world didn't question. She hated her legacy and didn't like people to know she was one of those who carried it. She felt like a victim, infected with the cause to carry on a name. At fifteen she told her father she would no longer be Elena, and he was moved softly to tears. He said her mother would turn in her early grave, that she would cry out in heaven for Elena to be the girl, the Sunlight she had given birth to. She had died, he told her, without ever acknowledging the full truth of Elena Ceausescu, and why should that legend be spoiled by the act of her only child?

Alina was upset, but her mind was made up. She told him she would be Alina because its sound echoed respect for her parents' decision, but it proved she had made a choice, like a strong woman does. Her father soon told her Alina was a beautiful eastern name, and she promised herself she'd love him forever. He never told her anything bad after that. He didn't describe a single day of his working life to her, and she understood.

Gogu was in debt beyond hope, and now Alina was the same, carrying on another harsh legacy of Elena Ceausescu and her mirrors and shoes, and her wines from the deepest cellars in France. When she was told she could visit him at his intensive care bedside in Bucharest, she used the last of her money to buy a ticket to the capital. There, as she approached his door with flowers in her hand, a grisly man waited. He knew she was coming, and he wanted to remind her she was falling deeper and deeper and that he was the one looking into the hole. He said he had been the one who had written to her, to remind her in his own firm way of her vital mission. He said she had a duty, like Gogu once had a duty, and she must discharge that duty.

In a little room just three doors away from her vegetative father, he told her of some men who would soon start to insist she begin making headway. They might, he said, come and prostitute her or abduct her or, he toyed, even kill her if she didn't cooperate. He said he'd make sure she had a nice headstone, courtesy of the state, on which her name would be the only sign that she'd ever been alive. It would read: *Here Lies Elena, Just Another Dead Romanian Elena.*

He told her to scram, to clear off and come back only when things were better. Her father, he said, would always be waiting. She had not seen him since the beating. She promised herself that she would only rush to his side if she gave up on The Policy. Quitting, she told herself, would probably be enough to get her threatened again, to get her hurt or raped or killed, but it might also allow her one last time to see the father she loved – a tragically naive, stupid hope that the only rock in her life could comfort her inside the very mouth of a fearsome fate.

GADAKA knew her desperation, her confusion. He felt it in her words and saw it in her body. It made her stand out among all the rich beauty of all the poor Eastern European girls he had seen. He had wooed her, talking to her like a counsellor, like a man who had the solution to her problems if only she would give him the time. She felt his longing and his kindness, but she knew enough about the men who asked her to do things that she knew his exotic, special, taboo tastes too. She knew she was a place he could turn to, a secret exit from his yearning, and she was sure that the men she had talked with, men like GADAKA, were not driven by violence, but by a misplaced lust. In a little way, she thought, he might be falling in love with her.

Beyond all that wavy, typical-Alina reasoning, she knew he was willing to pay. His wallet had opened to her for hours online and she felt it when she used her card and real money came out of the machine. GADAKA promised Alina – *you say Aleeena like this xx* – that he had the money to lift her into a new life. It was a sum of money which would have all but cleared her father's debts and opened the safe door to his bedside. To her, GADAKA – whatever his identity, whatever rules he followed – was one of life's awkward and misunderstood heroes, just like her own father. It was a kind of secret.

He met her on the corner of the street named after Christmas Day. He was wearing a blue shirt of thick cotton, jeans and Reeboks and looked like a man from the West in the East – dressed down, but all going well. He had a small suitcase, a full head of good, sandy hair, white teeth and forty years of life. He tilted his head to the side when she walked up the street, and she knew it was him. She saw his eyes moisten when she got closer. She thought he looked at her like he loved her. Her big smile welled up from her stomach and took control of her face. She tucked her overnight bag back further up on her shoulder and felt awkward that she might not have dressed well enough.

He said: 'Alina. Oh Aleeeeena.' She laughed and he held out his hand for her to shake it.

She said: 'You don't shake hand with Romanian girl,' and laughed again.

He withdrew it, put it in his pocket and said: 'I'm sorry. I just want to touch you.' She laughed again.

'Call me Gad,' he said. This time she giggled. This was the man who would surely take her virginity. She would have lied if she had said that hadn't excited her a little bit.

He had already called a taxi and it arrived seconds later. The driver took off without a word, before asking GADAKA to just point when he wanted to turn. GADAKA did, ordering twists into random streets, chalking up a string of random angles through Iasi, checking behind him and smiling every few minutes as Alina was slipped from one side of the shiny back seat to the other. They drove for twenty minutes as he told her how pretty her city was, and that he had always wanted to see St Parascheva. Alina told him she was a wonderful woman and that she would be happy to bring him to her side. She protects Iasi, she said, and the whole region around it.

They alighted, leaving a large tip, at Union Square and took another taxi from which he looked all around him again. The taxi ferried them to an apartment building on a side of town she didn't know well. GADAKA tipped generously again, and as they entered the building, he told her she had beautiful skin, which was a true thing to say. The beautiful skin blushed.

He had hired a large one-bedroom apartment with a high ceiling and a fine view of the spires of the city, its grey tower blocks far in the distance, demoted by a big blue sky. He uncorked a bottle of wine and she spoke about how her English was improving and it was because of men like GADAKA. He wouldn't let her talk about the men, but asked her had she met any of them before. She said no. She said she was a virgin before she had even thought about the words. She hoped he didn't mind.

GADAKA showed his money, a bundle of crisp US dollars in an envelope, and put it on top of the television. He said he had arranged for a woman to deliver fresh food and drinks to the door whenever he called, and that he had thought of everything. She must not worry about a thing, he told her. Alina said she wasn't hungry, not wanting to feel the need to gorge herself like a starving Romanian in front of this most important man who had flown to her side from London. He told her she would get hungry, and she said she had already eaten. He told her, firing a shockwave through her body, that she would get hungry because she was going to be in this room for Eight Days.

He asked her to show him what she had bought with the money he had already paid her. Her hands shook as they removed little second-hand skirts, and bras and socks and knickers from her bag. He seemed pleased with her purchases and took them from her, laying them out in a line of uniforms in front of him. He took clothes from his own bag, adding, mixing and matching to the six outfits which fed his strongest desires. He removed, finally, a white wedding dress and told Alina that he felt so lucky that he was going to play with a girl as sweet as she.

When settled with these arrangements, he told her he was going to explain how it was going to work and that she must listen with great care. She put everything in her mind to the side and tuned in, her big brown eyes focused on his face, her eardrums racing to get the words to her brain, it running to translate them and tell her what was going on as fast as it could.

He said she was now an employee and he had the right to sack her any time he chose. She must, he said, do her best and comply with his will. His happiness, he said, would bring her the happiness she deserved.

She would live in a nine-foot square, the boundaries of which he marked in the centre of the brown carpet with a roll of white masking tape. She would not leave the square unless he gave her permission.

Alina would begin Day One by giving him her whole life. She would dress as a toddler, a little girl not long on her feet, who needs commands and has learned that she gets fed, not when she cries, but when she asks. She would speak as a toddler, exactly as a toddler, baffled by the words she used, physically confused by his instructions.

On Day Two, she would be a little girl, a happy little dancer, jumper and singer who wants to do nothing but impress those around her. She would want to see dogs and horses and elephants and she would want to draw a stick man and say it was a man she knew and loved.

Day Three, she'd be approaching puberty, growing interested in her body, feeling sensations that made her want to be a grown-up. She'd say dirty words, smoke and cough and want to rid herself of childish things.

On Day Four, she'd be mid-teens, strutting around with shapely legs and cute breasts, willing to drink whatever was cool, no matter how sick it would make her. She'd be cheeky, unapologetic and know that no one knows the world like she does.

Five, she'd live out the first day when a boy fumbles with things which ignite him, a day when she's drunk and ill. She'll later want to go to a party and get more drunk and think how it would be soft and kind to feel the intimate touch of another girl.

Six, she'd be her own age, an eighteen-year-old streetwise, sexy girl, full of life and faith and hate and hurt, but she'd be different from most others. She'd be fully trusting of an inspiring man, a caring man, a companion who enters her dreams and talks of true love.

On Seven, she'd rest, eat, drink, relax and be occasionally free to leave the square. And later, he told her, his face straight and serious, she would marry the man who has protected her all her days. He would take her to the bedroom and impregnate her with a child to love and adore.

And on Eight, he told her, he would leave. He had a plane booked for that night and he would walk out in the morning. She would stay until he left, and twenty minutes after that, she would be free to go. He added, looking away from her, that there was something she would have to do that morning, but that it wouldn't take long.

'Do,' he asked, a strange colour in his cheeks, 'you understand?' She tried to think of something to ask which might make her sound like a professional, but she couldn't. She said: 'Dah. I say Yes.'

GADAKA continued, firing out the words like a prepared speech, confusing and muddling her, making her work so hard already: 'You will seek my permission each time you leave the square, and that will only be because you need the bathroom. If I want you to wash, I will tell you. Each time, you will be given a set number of minutes in which you are allowed to use the bathroom, but you will not have privacy. You will be handed your food when you deserve it. You will always be thinking of your role, of me and how much you love me. You will not cry unless it is part of your role. You will perform for me like you are a professional and you will at no stage cause me to remember that I am paying you for your work.

'If at any time I feel that you are unhappy with this situation, I will leave. At no stage will you be in danger. And at all times you will be called Martha. It is, from this moment, your one true name. Do you have any questions?'

There was nothing Alina could think of, so she shook her head. 'No,' she said, pausing. 'No, I have not questions.' Eight Days.

GADAKA smiled, walked over and stroked her face. 'That's a good girl,' he said. 'Very good girl.'

Alina did not feel sick. She didn't curl her face up in disgusted surprise at the weight of his depravity, she didn't consider saying that this was way beyond what he had suggested she would do and she didn't want to bring up the possibility of a renegotiation. They were both in the room now, and they both needed each other. There was an agreement and it could be done. One day, she thought, she will look back on this with her own child in her arms and she will whisper that she once did something truly ugly to make such love and beauty possible. Her child would only ever hear good things. Not even her husband would know. He would just smile at her when they visited Iasi and heard people say *there goes Alina, there's no one to replace her.*

She knew no one would come looking for her, wonder where she was or ask someone if she was okay. Her father would not worry and phone the police, her neighbours would not notice that the quiet girl in trouble with an official wasn't there and the men who regularly watched her living her life would go online as normal and find another Alina to regulate. She felt it was as if she could walk out at any time, but she had nowhere to walk to. She knew that she would do whatever it was she had to do, and that in Eight Days she would be free. The journey she had embarked on with The Policy as her guide had entered a new and testing phase, but it was still the same journey. The hardest part of any hard fight, she told herself, must be the final round. When it was all over, she would sleep and awaken and live, really live, for the first time. This vile Eight Days sentence will be served, and then she will be alive.

That night GADAKA retired to his room at 10 p.m. Alina sat in the square – her new workplace – and tried to conjure up images of the big, bright future which was so close that she could count the days on her bony fingers. She would go and see her father, do something for him, help him or kiss him or sing to him, and she would pay the official who wanted nothing from her but money. She would leave and travel to England and America and meet and eat and love and laugh with that good, honest husband. Alina wondered what he would look like, and couldn't help thinking of the shy, kind face of Henry Sender.

She didn't leave the square that night. She didn't get up and check the door or pick up the envelope crowning the television and flick through the money. She didn't think about stealing it. She didn't urinate or eat or even make a sound. She just lay down, closed up into herself and thought how it must be possible to rid her conscience of any kind of secret shame she will leave this apartment with. Alina slept deeply, uncovered on a hard carpet, and dreamed only good things.

GADAKA began his week with Alina like a man begins a week of work. He studied his project, considered it, walked around it, digested it and planned how he would conquer it. He seemed uneasy at first, slow to act, perhaps cautious of what he had before him, or of what he had within. But he would change as the days went on. He would become something remarkably different from the man she had met on the street, and Alina wondered, her body sore, her conscience confused, if he was two men sharing one heart. After he had put her to bed in her square that second night, drunk from what she had been forced to drink, he whispered promises to her which she did not understand. He took to his own bed soon after, an ache starting in his testicles, an ache ending the day. He groaned in pain for more than an hour. She thought he was having a nightmare, and wondered what could scare him in his dreams. She watched the sunrise with her head on the floor, tilted to the side.

Alina considered how it had seemed more like a year than a week by the time Martha climbed into a white dress which was too large and smelled of mothballs. At the same time, GADAKA put on a tuxedo which no longer fitted. The couple stood in the square and she said she did, she would, she will marry him. He opened the fridge and they drank champagne, hers – he thought it was so funny – through the veil, and he then sipped from the same glass in yet another act of true love. She was taken to the luxurious marital bed, and her husband asked Martha to pray with him to God for thanks as he filmed her with a video camera, her veil lifted from her face, her lips moving in solemn honesty. Later, she lay still in her wedding dress as her husband lifted it and, crushing her ribcage, dripping saliva into her face, told her she would never leave him because she had proved that she loved him. He said then that he loved her, rolled off and drifted away to sleep.

She made not a sound some hours later when he woke, angry, shouting about sluts and bitches, and kicked her out of his bed. She lay trembling on the floor, waiting for his next move. When it didn't come, she tried to shift her body into a place and shape which would allow her see the sunrise. She watched it through a stained veil.

At the end of her days, she washed and showered as ordered. And when she was done, he reminded her there was something he wanted her to do before he left. He asked her to consider what had happened here, that she had slept with a man who did not use protection. She only began to understand what he meant when he told her that he wanted her to think about the fate of their imaginary child – its fate in this room, with this man. Alina cried some time later, a real cry from her real soul. But she was so afraid to disobey him she made it sound like the helpless cry of an infant.

Sometime around 10 a.m., as she sat in silence, her days all counted and counted again, GADAKA left. He said nothing when he emerged from the bedroom with his suitcase packed. He didn't even look at her as she looked at him, noting how he now looked clean and smart, like a businessman from the West in the East, wearing a suit she had never seen before. He walked across the room, walked around the border of her square and out of the door, leaving nothing but a trail of aftershave in his wake.

Alina looked to the television and the fat envelope. She sat there for eight minutes, sometimes trying to work out if this was really all true, sometimes wiping the tears from her face. She stood up and, before anything else, she showered, trying to clean a new smell from her skin. But it didn't seem to go, so she kept on washing. She smelled her hands and her arms, but it was as if it was stuck to her. She scrubbed fast at her breasts and belly and body. She washed her mouth out over and over again. She hurt more than she ever thought she could. Tears of pain and shame mixed in with the hot, hard water as Alina tried to erase Eight Days from her life.

Raw and silent, businesslike and swift, she dressed in the clothes she had been wearing when she arrived, put the rest of her things in her bag, put it over her shoulder and went to the television. She stopped. She looked out of the window and onto her city, at the spires of the church which held the bones of St Parascheva, and then to the envelope. The church, the envelope. She reached out and laid her hand on its bulk. It was full, heavily rich. She picked it up and saw and touched, for the first time ever, a massive one-hundred-dollar bill. Behind it was nothing but clippings from English newspapers announcing to the world the names of some people who had recently died.

13

A squeak, a thud and a shake as the back door is slammed closed. Della and Rosie light up, smoke rising and flavouring the air. It's a warmer, calmer day, the sun free to brighten the world as the fresh breath of Mother Nature, her scent and promise, caresses the land. Such pleasantness means little to Rosie and Della.

Says Rosie: 'You're a stupid cunt.'

'Fuck off. How was I to know they were at the door?'

'By lookin through the glass, you dick. They know we're here nigh.'

'Who is it?'

'I don't fucken know. Probably the fucken peelers about Robert again.'

'Fuck's sake. Why don't they just ring if they get any news?'

'Dunno. Where's Mummy?'

'Dunno.'

Cigarettes are flicked in unison. A lengthy pause, and some tuts. Rosie speaks. 'So Muck's spotted a motor?'

'Aye, he toal me last night.'

'Wee boy-racer thing, is it?'

'No. It's a van.'

'A VAN?'

'Shhhhhhh.'

'Fuck's sake. A fucken van? Who wants a fucken van?'

'We do. We're goin to travel.'

'Aye right.'

'Fucken are.'

'Aye right. Do youse think you're the fucken A-Team or somethin?'

'Fuck up. We can live in it if we get stuck. Muck's near raised enough money for it nigh.'

'Right.' A pause. 'You're fucken serious then?'

'Aye. Fuck this hole. Too many fucken bad memories.'

'Hmm.'

Della stares into the sky, at something that catches her attention. She pauses, and then: 'What the fuck is that?'

'What?'

'That there, hangin there. It looks like a big spider or something.'

'Fuck, I'm twistin me neck here. I can't see. What is it?'

An oily golden object dangles on a greasy black string in front of Della's eyes. Its form is caught occasionally by the sun, and it glints, as if winking at her. Della's eyes scan the length of the cord. She thinks it's some kind of natural webbing, but she can see no creature. It is dangling from within the hole in the steel wall above. Rosie shrugs, turning back round to adopt her usual stance, tugging hard on her cigarette. Della reaches out and feels the object, its cold, wet hardness, its fulsome weight telling some kind of story. She looks up again to the hole and tugs quickly at the object. The thread breaks easily. The object is in her hand. She wipes it clean.

She says: 'Am I fucken mad or is that gold?'

'Wise up, Del. Stupid bitch.'

'Fuck. Is it someone's tooth?'

'Wha?'

She holds it up, a finger running over it. 'What does that look like to you?'

'Don't be fucken disgustin.'

Della runs the object around in her hand again, shrugs and puts it into her pocket. She looks up at the little cotton cord, black and greasy, its pieces bonded firmly together with a thick, sticky goo, blowing in a soft breeze she cannot feel. She finishes her cigarette.

'I'm away in,' she says.

'Aye,' says Rosie. 'Me too. You think them cunts are still at the door?'

'Wait till I read their minds and I'll tell you.'

'Fuck up.'

Frank the Fess no longer feels any pain. He is fully numb, his nervous system shutting down, his body freed from ache. He has found a kind of contentedness, a slight smugness that he has resolved something, that he has started to make a peace with himself.

He knows now that he has been kidnapped by a man given to extremes and figures that he's been placed in an empty, disused, customised oil tank in a back yard. The yard faces east; the house, west. It's small and untidy, with little room for anyone to manoeuvre. As seen in some terraced city streets, the oil tank sits on a raised steel frame flush with the back wall of the house, the area beneath extending the cramped Victorian space. Frank believes that the tank itself used to be home to an illegal and ferocious fighting dog called NAILER, an animal hidden from view by its owner and kept angry, muzzled and hungry between lucrative, horrible bouts.

One of the man's daughters, Della, is not happy in this house. She is involved with a young lad who was driven to an uncharacteristic and extreme act against her father and his dog. He is called Muck, and he killed NAILER by shooting a bullet into the tank, before turning the gun in anger on the back door of the house. But he only shot at the top, for fear of harming his lover. The uncertain success of killing NAILER did not satisfy him. Muck later launched a fresh attack on the man, crushing his testicles under the blow of a sledgehammer. This has left the man permanently damaged. Muck took this dangerous course after his own newborn baby disappeared, allegedly stolen by gypsies. But mild-mannered Muck perhaps heard a rumour that transformed his loss to rage. His sensibilities left him as he turned, hammers and guns and revenge on his mind, to the wild man who had already assaulted him for standing with his daughter. The rumour exonerated the gypsies and suggested that the man, in a crazed fit of anger, may have taken his own daughter's newborn baby and given it to the merciless NAILER. The infant was probably fed to the dog alive, bawling and helpless, to save the man from having to kill the child with his own mad hands. Della has either not heard the fierce rumour or she will not accept it, locking it away in a room in her mind, trusting the innocent certainty that no grandfather would feed his grandchild to a dog. Muck, forever fresh bruises from his own father's hands on his face, may have a more realistic view of the infinity of betrayal.

The police are suspicious, treating the case as that of a missing person, and they have little evidence to suggest that the child was murdered. But they are keen on pressing the matter with the absent parents of these girls, coming round to drink tea and eat chocolate and talk sympathetically in the hope that some new clue will emerge as to the fate of the little boy. They've even, on at least one occasion, searched the house, but not very effectively, failing even to find that piece of evidence which proves the baby is dead. The sole remnant of the child lies in a place which the father of the house would have called his own, where he ended a child's life and nurtured a dog for pain. Frank knows that he has met this man, that he was put in this dark hole by his hands. He has no memory of the event. He has no memory of the man, but he's sure the man will be disposed to wreak a terrible and limitless revenge on young Muck at some point in the future. He believes that now it is only a matter of short hours before Muck and Della leave Belfast, and he is certain that the young lad will be proposing to her with a cheap, shiny wedding ring in the days to come.

Frank had used a bone from a baby's leg to prise the lone crown from the side of his mouth. It hadn't been too difficult. The crown was strong, but the tooth within and the gum around were weak. He hadn't felt much pain. He had held the extracted metal to his one ray of light, wiping the blood from its golden sheen, before beginning to tie it to the thread. Sunk into that metal, as any cursory examination would reveal, was one brilliant, 0.5-carat diamond, worth a great deal more than the material in which it was embedded. It would be enough to get two decent young people away from a place they should no longer be, to give them a chance to find a home elsewhere, to find a new leaf and turn it. It would be enough to see them right when they again created a child.

Frank's certain the jewellery will be in Muck's hands shortly. Muck will appreciate that it may have value and he knows people who can check it out for him. And Frank knows exactly what Muck will do with the money. The jewels are better with the youngsters than with him. You can't take it with you, he thinks.

For the last thirteen minutes Francis M.N. Cleary has been trying to turn over, onto his side. It's a struggle, but then it's all been a struggle of late. He hasn't got much left within him. He was not going to survive another day in this place, and he wasn't interested in doing so anyway. What would happen if he was rescued? Straight to hospital to assess the damage, to calculate the amount of toxins which had soaked into his skin? Intensive treatment, drugs and more immobility? Have his mind played with, doped and turned to alien thoughts and processes and moods? Then what? Back to the nursing home? Back to that bed where Rhonda would nip ever harder at his thin ankles every day? No thanks. He had passed on a baton of hope, and he had at least diluted the guilt which tortured him.

He's now on his side, a sudden rush of power allowing him to flip up and lie in a position he has not been in since he was placed in the tank by a man who must have known he would die there. He closes his eyes and falls over, flat onto his face, his mouth open into the sludge. He tries to breathe, to eat, to take the dead fuel a little into his dry self, hastening his end, and he dies, suffocating, drowning. A little thread is wrapped around the index finger of his right hand. Clutched in that fist, where he knew it will one day be found, is enough evidence to crack the case of the missing baby called Robert: one tiny, tooth-scarred tibia.

My dear old friend,

They have relocated me. That's what they called it. They say I am burning down my own house and that I am a danger to myself. Two men came to get me. What could I do? I ask you, what could I do?

They put me in a little room in a nursing home. It's nicely decorated. It was Detective Sergeant Ryan who contacted Social Services to report me. I can't blame him. He's a good man.

There is a woman here, a nurse, called Rhonda. Her real name is Rita, I was told, but she doesn't like it. She has some psychological problems, I can tell. She pours glasses of water onto me while I am in bed, and then tucks me up. It's unpleasant. She has also taken to nipping at my ankles. It is interesting in one way. I don't like her, but I am sad for her all the same. I call her Rita, and it winds her up.

Have I considered trying to communicate to others what she is doing? Yes, you fool. But you know that I cannot infect or destroy anything else, that I am past caring about myself. I must suffer now, it is my time, my due. It is richly deserved. Perhaps Rita has been sent from God.

My house was sold. A percentage of the money has gone towards my care. I couldn't think of what to do with the rest of it. I opted to have it turned to jewellery so I could at least keep it with me, away from the greedy hands of others, while I ponder. Charity? Animals? Children? Victims? It is in the form of a dental crown. I know I cannot lose it. Rita doesn't know about it. I never smile whilst she is attending to me.

I don't think I will see the Fan again. He no longer wanted to talk with me because of the confessions, and he came around to tell me so. He said that he had decided that I had definitely gone too far. He stared at me for a long time. I wasn't scared. I told him that I had a confession. I said that The Last Door, that becoming a Provider and Denier, that owning everything, was an enormous, towering pile of shit. I told him the interviews with anonymous thugs and gangsters in the book were all made up, that it was all a fantasy from a former psychology teacher who pulled out every stop to get a tiny toehold in academia, but became nothing more than a mascot, an old fool with a worthless message. I said I was a cheat, a liar, and that he had been cheated and lied to. I said that even the letters, the M.N. of my name, were invented. I told him it meant nothing, that it was My Nonsense.

I said I had published the book myself, that I had no appropriate qualifications, only a string of stupid courses and letters to my name. I told him that it was all nothing and nothing and nothing.

He walked away, dejected. Perhaps he will turn back to God. Surely he really does need to deal with what he has done, to confess? Surely to God? No vessel can hold that in, surely? IT BURNS INSIDE.

My little dog did finally return, but not for long. Before they took me away, I was allowed to contact Detective Sergeant Ryan. He took my call and his voice was sorry. I explained that he had not considered my dog in all this. He said he would fix it. He promised me. He came to see me yesterday. I couldn't believe I had a visitor. He brought my little dog with him and it was a joyous reunion. He had taken him to his own house and given him a home there. Both seemed very happy. He's bringing him in again next week. Will I be raising my incarceration problems with him? Do not be a fool. His good conscience is already a burden.

Do you think I should inform Detective Sergeant Ryan about the wealth in my teeth? I think I might, if I see him again. He would know what to do with it on my passing.

Regards, old friend,

Francis Cleary

14

It's been hell trying to get Shuff out of the bar. One drink and ten minutes became four drinks and twenty-seven minutes. Henry's gone from drunk to terrified to oddly satisfied to terrified to drunk to furious, and they were all unwelcome. Now Shuff is laughing into his face.

'Chill fucken out,' he says, pumping second-hand narcotic and old pizza fumes from his tubby mouth.

Henry's had enough. He can understand how Shuff's a good guy to have around when there's trouble, even if he does bring it on himself. But the rest of the time he's a useless big, smoking, boozing, snorting, snoozing, hungry Irish shite. He puts a hand up to the face of the big man, USA-style.

'Talk to the hand,' he says. 'I'm going.'

'Hen.' Shuff downs another vodka. 'It's a jungle out there, big lad.'

'You're supposed to be fucking working for me.'

'Aye.'

'And?'

'Aye. You're right. I hate having to do fucken shite when I've got the thirst.'

'You've always got the thirst.'

'Anno. Pain in the arse.'

'You know, Shuff, I think you're just fucking obsessed with breaking every rule you can. You and that Last fucking Door.'

'You're obsessed with finding fucken rules.' Shuff wags a

thick finger. 'And you make plenty of them up too, by the way. Fuck's sake.'

'You coming or not?'

'Aye. Balls hurt, so they do. Can't walk the best. Blew a load round that wee slapper's face, so I did.'

'That's one way to put it.'

'Aye.'

'Come on.'

'Right, big lad.' Shuff tips the remaining dribble of vodka into his body, stands up, an ache on his face, and fixes his testicles with a grunt. 'Fuck me sideways.'

'Come on, Shuff. Taxi time.'

Shuff puts a hand up to Henry, turns around and bow-legs his way to the bar. It's the last straw. Henry's foot kicks out at a chair, startling other customers. He wants to kick Shuff. He's speechless. He's not going to pay him after this crap. Tender fists clench and Henry prepares to leave by himself. Shuff turns around from the bar and holds up a bottle of vodka like a prize. He opens it as the barman gives him his change.

'Couldn't resist,' he says on his return. 'Fucken prices are diabolical.'

'Okay. Fine. Now come on.'

The taxi driver, while monitoring Shuff as he downs raw vodka in the back of his cab, takes the pair to one of six grim, grey, badly lit tower blocks on a street one mile from the city centre. He checks Henry's printout again, and nods that he's sure this is the right place. They alight – Shuff slapping the driver on the shoulder and informing him that his granda was Russian and communist as fuck – and stand on the pavement, looking up.

'Tenth floor,' says Henry. 'I hope she's in.'

It's 2.02 a.m.

'Tenth floor?' says Shuff. 'I hope the fucken lift's working.'

He takes a swig and looks all around. The street is dead quiet. It feels as if there's no life here at all. 'I hope she's a fucken insomniac, big lad.'

'Yeah. She'll be fine. She's, well, she'll be fine about it.'

'If she's there.'

'If she's there. Only one way to find out.'

The main front door of the block is supposed to lock securely, but there's no lock on it at all. Shuff holds it open and Henry cracks a smile from somewhere as he enters the building. There's one lift, and from the outside it looks as if it's about the size of a telephone kiosk. It's out of order.

'Fuck that,' says Henry. 'Come on. Stairs.'

'Shite in a blue bucket,' says Shuff.

'You've faced worse.'

'I don't know about that.'

The stairway is dark and narrow. Random, half-hearted graffiti dots the walls. The men stop after the third flight, two heads pounding and four lungs stretching. They take the balance of the floors, Shuff pulling on his litre of vodka for sustenance, Henry running pictures of Alina through his mind. He's excited. The feeling is tempered by pictures of his former foster mother, but of all the times to think about her, this is not one of them. It takes them nine hard minutes to reach the tenth floor, each as exhausted as each other. Henry wonders why he had never noticed himself becoming so unfit. Her flat is number 103. The door is light green and ugly.

'This it?' gasps Shuff, bending down, hands on knees, balls aching.

'Yeah.' Henry wants to wait for a moment to catch his breath. He'll need it if he's finally going to see Alina in the flesh. 'Shuff?' he says.

'What?'

'Be nice to this girl, okay? She's a bit special.'

'No worries. Nice looking?'

'Fuck. Too nice for words, mate.'

'Happy days.'

'Shuff. She's not a hooker or communist or drug-dealer or anything like that, okay?'

'Don't you worry, Henry. I'll be good as gold. Sure, if everything's all right, maybe I'll just fuck off and leave you to it. You could do with getting your hole.'

'Well, let's see. Fuck knows who's in here.'

Henry knocks the door. No answer.

Shuff: 'Knock harder, fuck's sake. You probably have to wake her up.'

Henry knocks harder. Shuff's fist joins Henry's and cracks off the door like four thrown rocks.

'Fuck's sake, Shuff. You'll wake the whole floor.'

'Henry. Fuck up.' Shuff knocks again. Nothing.

'Shit,' says Henry.

'She ain't there, big lad. Unless she's hiding.'

'Why would she hide?'

'Dunno. What'd you know about her?'

'Well, she's in a bit of trouble. Debt, I think. Maybe she is hiding.'

'Right. Want the door put in?'

'No.'

'Then we have to go.'

'No.'

'Then are we going to hang out here all night like wankers?'

'No.'

'Okay, Henry, decision time. Tick tock. All work and no play makes Shuff a dull cunt.'

'Okay. The door. Can you do it quietly?'

'No. But I can do it quickly.'

Shuff steps back with a grimace and fixes his balls. Henry turns away. He doesn't want to look. This can't be right, doing this. There's a crash and a crack as the door is smashed open and whacks against an inside wall. Henry turns and notices how it almost came off its hinges. There's no immediate sign of interest from any other flat. Shuff offers Alina's home to Henry, and he walks in, heart drumming.

Henry switches on the light. The flat is tiny and, like the door, painted a sickly, light hospital-green. There's a bed in what might be called a small living room, and two tiny, empty, pawned bedrooms. She has designed herself a bedsit, a little box in which to live. There's a little kitchen area. One glass. One plate. Both washed. There's a picture of a glorious sunrise on a mantelpiece. Below, there's just wall where a fireplace never was. There is a computer on a desk beside the bed. On a patch of wall over the bed is a square of wallpaper on which teddies and rabbits run around.

A wheeled office-type chair is parked against one wall, underneath a window which looks out onto the grey towers across the street. To one side of the desk, behind the computer, from the centre of the ceiling, she hangs. The cord of her webcam is wrapped tightly around her neck and fixed to the light fitting. Her mouth is partly open. No one of any reasonable weight would have enough support from that light to hang themselves, but Alina had no bulk. She's been dead for a while. Days, probably. Her eyes are partly open. She's wearing cheap jeans and a white T-shirt. Somehow she looks stunning, like some confusing beauty from a bizarre pop video. The two men stand in silence.

'Well, now you know,' says Shuff, swigging.

'Fuck,' says Henry. He feels cold. He takes in the scent of her life for the first time. It's kind of musty. It's death. It's the end of the point of everything this was about. It's like coming to the end of a flight of fancy and learning it was all just stupid. What was it? Two nights on the piss with Shuff? One ultimate moment of shock at walking into this flat? One girl losing her face, another losing her life? What's it been about? What the fuck? What's the point? This is insane.

Henry sits on the bed. He puts his head in his hands and starts to weep. Shuff watches him. He shakes his head, sorry for his young friend. He pulls back the chair from the wall, to where Alina had kicked it in the last act of her life, and stands on it. He comes level with her face, wheels ready to slip. He looks into her eyes. Henry looks up.

'She liked you, big lad,' says Shuff. 'I can tell these things.'

Henry thinks this is stupid. He doesn't want any sympathy from this man. He stares at Shuff, stuck for a string of words, the sum of his thoughts. Shuff smiles at him, then at Alina. He kisses her.

'Hard lips,' he says. 'Bad diet.'

'For fuck's sake, Shuff.'

'Sorry.'

'Jesus Christ.'

'All right, all right. You'd never even met her.'

'I knew her. I'd spoken to her. I knew her.'

'Spoke?'

'Spoke.'

'On the phone?'

'Email.'

'Fuck's sake. So you never even heard her voice then?'

'Shut up.'

'Anyway, she's a looker. Like you said. I'd say she's looked better, to be honest.'

'Shut the fuck up.'

Henry wells up with tears again. Is she dead because of him? Has he killed someone? Shuff gets down from the seat.

It hadn't dared run from underneath him.

'You want me to take her down?' he asks.

'No. Leave her in peace.'

'Ack, I'm not bothering her.'

'Shut up, Shuff.'

'I'm fucken starving. D'you reckon there's anything to eat in this joint?'

'How the fuck would I know? How the fuck can you have an appetite now?'

'Munchies.' A pause. 'I'd love some fucken cheese.'

Shuff wanders over to the kitchen area and flips open the tiny fridge. It's not switched on. Inside are photographs, snapshots Alina wanted to be able to see, but didn't want to see her. Pictures of her father, of her father with Ceausescu, of her father with her mother, of her with her parents, of fairs and school and blurred yellowish images, naive pictures of the sunrise. One, in a glass frame, is a picture of her at the side of St Parascheva, Protector of Iasi.

'Fuck's sake,' says Shuff, flipping through cupboards, opening a drawer and pushing one lone large pan out of the way to see behind it. 'She didn't leave much.'

Henry wipes at his tears. He must stop crying. He can't allow himself to wade into tragedy. It would invite in Matilda, those heavy thoughts of his former foster mother that are demanding ache. And it would open the door to Alina, to letting free his full feeling for her. He knows she can make him feel sadder than he ever thought he could. Too much grief is waiting for him to take ownership. He knows it will want him to despair, to break, to consider taking his own life. This, he thinks, is an opportunity his mind has always sought – but Henry's not going there. He is not. He sits up and breathes out. He sees the pan, once filled with potatoes, and looks away. He won't look at it again. He looks at Shuff, moulding his testicles and drinking and owning everything he sees.

Says Shuff, turning to catch Henry's eye, his fruitless search at an end: 'You've never seen a body before, have you, Hen?'

'No.'

Shuff leans against a wall, silent for a moment. 'There's nothing to it. Dead as fuck, that's all.'

Henry's eyes squeeze tight. He's not sure if there are any more tears in there. He wipes them again. They have stopped. He breathes in deep and looks up. 'You don't care, do you, Shuff? You really just don't give a shit.'

'About what?'

'Alina. Or that girl at the club. The guy on the floor. That barman. Anybody. Do you?'

Shuff shakes his head, dismissive of Henry. He wanders back to the kitchen area, swigging on his juice. He looks again into the open cupboards.

'Shuff,' Henry says it again, this time louder. 'You just don't give a fuck, do you?'

The man walks back to the wall, beside the door, and leans against it again. He takes Henry's eyes as he swigs, holding them as the bottle lowers, a hand gripped hard on its neck.

'Not really,' he says. 'I told you all that, Hen. I've no ... you know.' He looks proud of himself. He smiles. He looks away. 'I've no conscience, big lad. Conscience is a coward.'

'So it's just you, is it? Just fucking you, just fucking Number One all the time.'

'Wha?'

'Just fucking Shuff Sheridan. That's all you're about.'

'All right, Hen.' Shuff shakes his head. 'Don't be getting cheeky now, big lad.'

'Just you. Only you.'

'You're grieving, Hen. Try to keep yer head on.'

Henry sits up, trying again to catch Shuff's eyes. 'How many people have you killed?'

'Wha?'

'How many? Two? Ten?'

'Wise up, Hen.'

Angrier. 'How many? Why would you have a problem saying? You're the one who's got life all sorted. You're the one who's not afraid of anything.'

'Aye, so they say.' A pause. 'I don't know. One or two.'

'Men? Women? Kids? What?'

Shuff shakes his head. He puts his free hand in his pocket, and swigs. 'Whatever, Henry.'

'And you've no guilt over it. You're telling me you have no guilt?'

Shuff looks to the cupboards again, as if he has seen something. He hasn't. 'Fuck guilt. Guilt is dead.'

'You're guilty now, Shuff. I can see it in your face.'

'Then you need yer eyes tested. Guilt is dead.'

'How many people have you killed? Come on. Sure, you've nothing to hide from anyone? You're the Provider and Denier. Things like that mean nothing to the likes of you. This dead girl hanging here means nothing.'

Shuff sniffs. Drug-flavoured mucus slides into his throat and he spits it onto the floor. 'Well, I've probably done in two or three cunts. That what you want to hear?'

'Come on, Shuff. Probably? Fess up now. Be brave.'

'Wise up.'

'Come on. Keep killing that conscience, Shuff Sheridan. Let it out.'

'Two or three. I fucken told you.' He shuffles his feet, clears his throat.

'What did they do to you? Call you names? Question your manliness?'

'Wise up.'

'Why did you kill them?'

'Wise up.'

'You're not so brave, Shuff. You're not brave enough to own up.'

Shuff takes in a deep breath and turns, looking into the distance, through a window, into the dark. He speaks: 'Back off now, okay? Back off.'

Henry's eyes drop to the floor, but he's not afraid. He's not scared of Shuff, not scared by a man who grows weaker as he grows stronger. He stares at scars on the tiled floor, little scrapes and marks, little traces of Alina's feet.

Shuff puts his vodka onto the floor and rubs his face. He says: 'Ever see a dogfight, Hen?'

It's a stupid question. 'Yes. Who hasn't?'

'A dogfight,' says Shuff. 'A real dogfight. Pit bulls.'

'Then, no. I wouldn't want to.'

'It's a brutal fucken thing, lemme tell you.'

'I know.'

'Y'see, I had this dog, called it NAILER. Fucken thing could fight for three hours straight. Cleaned a fucken fortune from the paramilitaries, from the UDA and all.'

'Good for you. I hope you had fun.'

'I did.' A pause. 'Y'know, I've had more run-ins with the paramilitaries than you'd believe.'

Henry believes. 'I believe,' he says.

'Well, a guy killed it on me. A wee prick who was shagging my daughter. He shot it.'

'Why did he do that?' Henry follows the patterns on the floor, wondering if Alina had sat here and looked at them too.

Shuff doesn't answer.

'Why did he kill your dog?'

Shuff shakes his head, whitewashing a memory, momentarily closing his eyes. He picks up the vodka again and swigs.

Henry looks up to him, and back to the floor. 'I don't care anyway,' he says. 'I don't care any more.'

Shuff holds his tongue, thoughts tumbling. Then he speaks, still staring into the night. 'Y'see, the fuckers could never work out where I kept him, you know. The dog. They wanted to nick him on me.'

'The paramilitaries?' Henry doesn't care. He thinks he should, that he should try harder to read these odd signals coming from Shuff, but apathy is too tempting right now.

'Aye.'

'Okay. So where did you keep him?'

'It was genius, like.' A pause. 'An oil tank, back of the house.'

'Pure genius. Maybe you should get a prize.'

'Then the other day I was pissed off and it just came to me. I thought, I'll get a guy and put the fucker in there.'

Henry looks up. 'Get who?'

'This man, right. This guy who was taking my shit, Hen. That's who.'

'Stealing from you?'

'Aye. Sort of.'

Henry looks back down. 'You're the thief, Shuff. From what I know, you're the thief and the arsonist and the murderer. Just my opinion, mate, but you're the last guy to judge others.' He looks back up. 'But then you're the Provider and Denier, eh?'

Shuff swigs and looks to the floor, then to the vodka in his hand. 'Three days ago.' He shakes his head, as if shaking something off, turns and saunters to the computer, fixing his balls. 'Is this on?' he asks.

'Three days ago what? When you put him there?'

'Wha?'

'You put him in there three days ago?'

'Aye.'

Henry looks to the floor again. Someone is trapped, he

thinks. What should he do? He has no idea. Apathy again. It weighs a ton, more than he had imagined it could.

Shuff swigs again, scanning the keyboard. 'Aye, he tried to take my shit, know what I mean?'

'No. I don't, Shuff.' He's growing bored with the riddles. 'I don't know what the fuck you mean.'

Shuff swigs. He fixes his balls. He wanders to the window and surveys the city lights again. Henry watches. He stands there for more minutes. Henry has never seen him so still for so long. He stays focused on the night.

Henry speaks. 'Do you want to do something about it? Ring someone?'

Shuff is still for a time. Then he turns and wanders back to the computer. Henry considers that Shuff might lash out, that he has stumbled from a path in his mind and might strike Henry on a whim. But the big man stops and punches only a button on the shut-down PC. His finger stays steady. 'I used to ride this secretary,' he says. 'She wanted to teach me all about computers and typing and all. Quick brown fox and all that bollocks.'

Henry nods. He almost laughs. 'You're just … something else, you know that?'

'I do.' Shuff meets his eyes. 'I know that.'

He turns and wanders back towards the window. He takes another swig. 'Right. End of story. So what's the plan?'

'The plan?'

'Aye. Wake up. What're we going to do?'

'I don't know. Just give me a while, okay?'

'Aye. Well look, there's no bother here. She's not going to cause any anyway. Fancy a pint? We'll drink to her.'

'No.'

'Suit yourself. I'm away, right? You staying here?'

'Do whatever you want.'

'I will. So you staying here?'

'I don't know.'

'I'll be back, right? I'm away to find a bar. Gaggin for a beer, so I am.'

'Right.'

'No funny business with the babe, right?'

'Okay.'

'She's dead gorgeous, so she is.'

'Yes.'

'Ring me if you need me.' Shuff reaches to a back pocket. 'Fuck. Forget that. Me phone's gone.'

Henry: 'I won't need you. Enjoy your drink.'

'I tell you, Hen, I'd love to see that Russian fucker again.' His eyes seem to glaze over. He puts down the bottle. 'By fuck, would I love that.' From somewhere inside, Shuff is reloading.

Henry nods. 'I bet you would.'

'See you later, big lad.'

'Bye.'

Henry had never been in a room with a dead body before. He had always feared the dead, although he had often been unable to stop himself thinking about them, their permanent peace, about joining their ranks. Now he is with death, looking at it hanging clear as light, light shining down onto it. He is surrounded by it, yet he is calm. Alina doesn't shock him. She wouldn't have wanted to. She's just dead. Gone and quiet, gone to where it's easier. The webcam, the teddies, the bunnies on the wallpaper, the sex toy she'd thrown away in case the police found it and scoffed – all instruments of an oppression which had passed.

A thought flashes through him when he looks to her again. His mind tells himself to be prepared if she suddenly opens her eyes, that he must run to her and take her down if she coughs or moves or jerks. But it was just another stupid thought, like all the stupid thoughts he'd come up with. He puts it to one side, and it disappears.

He spits now onto his hands and wipes them through his hair, ready for his next move. He pulls the chair to the computer and sits down, Alina's little square feet in the top corner of his eye, behind the monitor, to the left hand side. He switches it on and it cranks and clunks and sighs as its screen comes to life. He looks at the icons on her desktop as the screen freezes and stumbles, trying to make itself work. He sees that it's basic and functional, a computer used by its owner for a single purpose. There's a lone Word document. It's called Henry. He looks to her, and clicks.

My dears Henry. I am sorry that I must no more do the job for you. There is things changing and this man has asked me to marry and bride for him. He is nice and like you, a man who cares that girls get happy!!! I must now join with him in his house and then maybe we move to United States country. I will am going to have baby and this job is not good when I get big belly!! I am accept this is the way for me because of how I feel inside of myself. Please not be angry or disappoint in me. You are good man and thank you. Please remove me from the woundlicker website and stop paying the kind dollars to my card. Yours with bigs heart!! Alina xx

The document had dated itself four days ago, at a moment when Henry was passing seemingly endless time in a lecture, and failing to understand anything that was being said. The letter was a lie, a draft never sent because it was untrue. Alina had not wanted to lie, nor to tell the truth. She had died, damaged, raped both East and West, having given a whole other life to her dream yet having failed herself again and again. After her time with GADAKA, she had lived with a conscience and a shame which were too heavy for her to carry. She hadn't even asked her Saint for protection from the man she thought was going to rid her of her debts. She felt she had asked GADAKA to do what he did to her. She had invited him in to take her. After all this, after feeling that she had got it all so wrong, she had accepted she was never going to win, that The Policy was a way to live but not a way out, and she had accepted that death was an exit from a deep predicament which no one understood. No one, she had believed, really cared. She had killed herself, and she had killed the foetal child she suspected, even feared, was growing inside her.

Henry logs on to the web, her password pre-programmed into her lonely terminal. He opens his own account and sends a global email, forwarding Alina's lies to all the girls who work on Woundlicker Dot Com. They are lies for him, personal, passionate untruths masking a misery she wanted to hide. For Henry, they confirm he once had a precious, warm relationship with someone he had never met, never spoken with and one that had ended in a way he had never imagined a relationship could. But now he wants to share them, to expose them, to give them a purpose. He wants the others to see what sweet words she had said to him, and then tell them the truth about sweet words. He wants to spread the news.

With all that's around him, all that's within, in this room at this time, his brain is at the edge of as dark a place as it has ever been. He types in the URL of a Northern Ireland news site.

> A man known to police as 'a serial confessor' was last night found dead in an old oil tank in the back yard of a Belfast house.

Eccentric 91-year-old Francis M.N. Cleary – dubbed 'Frank the Fess' – had been missing for three days before an anonymous tip-off led the search to the disused container.

It's thought the former lecturer was kidnapped and put into the oil tank alive. Cleary, who sparked minor controversy with his alternative philosophy study *The Last Door*, had recently claimed responsibility for a string of crimes. Police sources now believe those offences may all have been committed by the same person.

A woman, known to be a member of staff at the nursing home where Cleary resided, has been arrested and was last night helping with enquiries.

In a statement, police representatives said they are urgently seeking Belfast ex-prisoner Digby 'Shuff' Sheridan (44) in connection with the grim find. It's believed Sheridan, who owns the property where Cleary's body was found, has recently left the country.

Police will not confirm a suggestion from a well-placed source that the bone of a small child was also found in the tank. It's known that Mr Sheridan's baby grandson Robert went missing six months ago and that police had been following up on anonymous allegations that he may have been stolen by travelling gypsies.

Detective Sergeant John Ryan said: 'This is a very sad case. Mr Cleary was a gentleman in his twilight years, and to have been kidnapped and locked up in this way is nothing short of obscene.'

He added: 'We're seeking Mr Sheridan as a matter of urgency.'

It is understood that the nursing home employee, who was one of the last people to see the former psychology teacher alive, was arrested after failing to answer questions. A handwritten journal implicating her in abusive behaviour against Cleary was found in the nursing home.

Police sources said the woman, who cannot be named for legal reasons, remained silent after her arrest.

Cleary's self-published book, *The Last Door*, bizarrely argued that some of history's most influential and infamous characters had purposely diluted and killed their own conscience in order to become more powerful. It claimed anyone could achieve the same, suggested how it could be done, and warned against it.

The book was condemned by many academics but was nonetheless a hit with students. Its aged author had gained a part-time university lecturing post outlining his controversial theory as part of a module on radical and cult philosophies, but that came to an end when he began confessing to crimes which he had not committed. The university has since distanced itself from Cleary's theories and actions.

Henry knows where Digby 'Shuff' Sheridan is. He knows he could have him brought to justice, that he could testify in court against him and have him locked up for life. He knows he could tell the stories that Shuff could never tell, that he could stand in court, facing Shuff, and reveal what Shuff would never reveal. But he knows now too that he won't be around to see any of that. He takes something positive from the thought that Shuff knows nothing about what's going on back home, and that he will not find out until he lands in London, where the police will bring him down. So be it.

But now he has work to do, he has a story to complete. He

stands on the chair beside Alina and gently lifts her lightness upwards, unwrapping the hard cord from around her neck. He takes her into his arms and steps down, holding her tighter to himself than he needs to do. She's cold and firm but her glassed, dry, chocolate eyes still shine from the light above. He lays her on the bed and reconnects the webcam. He logs into Woundlicker Dot Com and creates a little square for himself under the name *Aleeena*. It makes him smile. He comes into view, moves the chair out of the way and sits on the bed beside her. He lifts her gently up so she sits stiff with him, leaning delicately against his side like a supported lover.

Men begin logging in to see what they can see of Alina. They see a live man flickering onto their screens and an ill-looking girl who does not move. Many are curious as to her wellbeing, and they're excited by the twist in this little square. They begin to ask Henry if he's going to fuck her, and some ask if she's dead. He pulls her closer and hugs her, tears well in his eyes again, as insane words flick into view. More and more log on as news spreads that there's something contorted going on, and the room fills with faceless, fearless men.

Henry reaches out and lifts Shuff's half-empty, half-full bottle of vodka and starts to sip. He writes nothing, watching the distant minds unwrap over a vision of something that isn't right, a live snapshot of death, a perversion they have not yet explored. Henry drinks more raw vodka than ever before and his head starts to spin. He glugs on it, holding Alina ever closer, sending out some kind of message to her deadness that she was loved – more loved, perhaps, now that she is dead than she had been while alive. This is what we have all done, he thinks, looking into the webcam which brought her image to him – we have all killed this beautiful young Romanian girl.

When he finishes the vodka, drunk and angrier, he lies her back onto her bed. He returns to his webmaster account, ready to write an email to his girls, to follow up on Alina's untrue letter.

> This is Henry. Woundlicker Dot Com will close. I will not provide this service any longer. I am sorry if this causes any upset. One of the girls has been killed. You have read her letter. It is not true. It was written at a time when she knew she was going to die. Her name was Alina. She was from Iasi. She met a client. He has killed her. All the clients have killed her. Goodbye. Henry.

The replies come pouring, roaring in.

> Henry what fuck????? This is not the thing now to do. Maybe she meet mad man etc but this is not a place to meet men for the real??!!!! This is my work Henry and I must make the money???!!! Selda

> Hi Henry. Please help me. This is my good job and I am best at it. I make regulars and have do no wrong. The people are not killing me and I never meet them like u rules ask. If she has met man then it is her problem not for me. Do not stop the site henry. Please please. I do anything!!! Ecaterina XX

> Mr Henry. Ok she kill but that is not site make her dead, no. I spoke alina from Iasi and she nice. I am sorry but life must keep go henry. Please no close the site. I have big problems and this is my help. Look me online now and see how me do!!!! Sabina XXXX

Henry falls asleep, his stomach aching and head thumping, right there on Alina's bed as she rests beside him, watching him, without blinking, being watched by men who wish they didn't have to.

He wakes, jumping and startled, as a shirtless Shuff comes bounding into the room, slamming the busted door shut, amazingly full of energy and songs of romance. He has a bottle of vodka in each hand and lipstick and a deep cut on his face. He has blood on his stomach, his arms. Someone else's blood. It's on his hands and his jeans. Aside from the red, his body is entirely blue. VIDERANDDENIERPROVIDER ANDDENIERPROVIDERANDDEN.

It's like a religious text, an unbroken mantra encasing him, punctuated only by fat nipples, a deep belly button and unexplained scars. Shuff's sweating, gasping but dancing and singing as he takes the centre of the room, performing in front of Henry's dizzy eyes.

'What the fuck about you, Hen?' he bellows. 'This town is fucken mental.'

Henry says nothing. He just watches this murderer of the very old and maybe even the very young relish his dead happiness of cheap drink and punched strangers. Shuff's eyes twist in and out, stoned on whatever it was that was in whatever room it was that Shuff walked into and took. He puts his head on one side. 'Okay, wee Hen? Cat got yer tongue?'

'No Shuff. I'm cool.'

'You are, ye boy ye. Cool as fuck.' Shuff finishes the last of one bottle and flings it into the corner of the room with a crash. Henry doesn't flinch. Shuff winks.

'How's our girl?' he asks. 'Were you tempted to finger her yet?'

'Afraid not.'

'Ack dear. Maybe she's frigid anyway. Geddit? Frigid. Hahaha!'

'I get it.' Henry unfolds the arms which had folded automatically when he awoke on Shuff's return. 'Good time?'

'Aye. Picked up a load of fucken mad speed in some wee dive up the town, so I did.'

'I bet you did.'

'Aye. Clocked some cunt to get it. You want to see him nigh. Eyes to the right, nose to the left. Know what I mean? Hahahaha!'

'I do.'

'You do.' A pause. He stands still. 'What the fuck's wrong with you?'

'What happened your shirt? The shirt.'

'Couldn't fucken tell ye, big lad. Memory blank. Must mean it's good gear. Want some?' He pulls a bag of powder from his pocket, spilling some onto the floor. 'Ooops,' he says. 'It's fucken mighty, so it is. Made in Romania, yer man said.'

'The man you stole it from?'

'Aye. He got chucked down a pile of stairs, so he did. Shame. Hahahahaha!'

'Yes, it is.'

'So you want some?'

'Yes. I'll have some.'

'Good lad. Fucken chilling out now you know the bitch is gone, so you are.'

'Yes. That's exactly what it is.'

Henry goes to Shuff, takes the unknown chemical from his hand and sits beside Alina, pouring it out onto the picture of the sunrise, lining it up with her only card and snorting it through an unspent, lonely one hundred dollar bill which had been tied around the neck of a little teddy bear. He feels a rush lift him out of himself, pulling upwards on his body, his face, making him smile, making him feel as if he could bounce from the bottom of the tower block to the top. It excites the watchers. He snorts more as Shuff uses the bathroom, pissing all over the floor and singing some kind of anthem. Henry is white, his eyes shaking and limbs vibrating, by the time Shuff emerges from the toilet.

'Fuck me,' he says, burping. 'Go easy, big lad. You're not used to that.'

'I am,' says Henry.

'You're not,' says Shuff.

'I've got a funny brain. It used to make me speed up. Made me feel like I do now, but it's not so bad.'

'Funny brain? What the fuck, like.' Shuff sits down on Alina's chair, watched by men who lick their lips in anticipation of some kind of horror. 'Your problem, Hen, is that you don't really know how to live.'

'Yes.' Henry's body races, but his mind is stone cold still. Then it sprints.

'You have to swallow everything life throws at you. Take it into you. Spend it. Know what I mean?'

'Yes.'

'No fear, Hen. Fear's just excitement, turned round. You just have to turn it round. That's when you know you've gone through that fucken Last Door.'

'Yes. Vodka.'

Shuff hands it to him, smiling.

'You just have to beat it all. Go through that Door, big lad. It's fucken mighty, so it is.'

'Yes.'

'Now get off the fucken bed. I've some business here with this wee lady.'

'Yes.' Henry stands up, feeling tall and strong and twice alive, and steps back. He knows what he's about to see and he's not afraid of it.

Shuff stands up, singing, and lifts Alina into his arms. He begins to kiss her on the lips, humming through his nose as his tongue pushes hard into her mouth, licking all around it. He lays her down as the online men grow more excited, now knowing she is a corpse. He pulls off her T-shirt and unclips her trousers, pulling them down to her knees. He climbs onto her, almost concealing her, licking her face.

Henry watches, as if defiled, as if raped, yet knowing and calm. The computer screen flickers with thrill as lines and lines of suggestions and demands flood in from keyboards around the world. Henry looks away from the obscenity in front of him. The watchers note his act, as they load up on Shuff's deeds. Henry can feel their eyes. He decides not to censor. He decides to deal this poison, perhaps his only way of further damaging the thirsty demons who drink it in.

One man, GADAKA, asks Henry why he doesn't charge. Henry stares at his words and GADAKA stares at him. Henry clicks on his webmaster's account and enters a code. It orders all the watchers to pay, or else it will boot them: $100 a minute. Cheap for Alina, he thinks, dead or alive. The chatroom is almost abandoned, left to six men addicted to depravity beyond reason. GADAKA tells him he should charge more. Henry hikes the price again, $200 a minute.

GADAKA tells him he's laughing out loud. He says he loves Alina. He tells him Alina was willing to do anything on screen, and on his hired floor in Iasi. Henry considers his words. GADAKA tells him Shuff has fallen asleep. Henry looks. Shuff lies half on top of her, beginning to snore. GADAKA wonders if Henry has ever fucked Alina. Henry says yes. He says everyone has fucked Alina. GADAKA laughs – *hahahahahahahaha*!

GADAKA says she was amazing, so good that he has pictures from the special day he married her. He asks who killed her? Henry tells GADAKA that he did, that we all did. GADAKA laughs again. He says he had been good to her, that she had met her end when he wasn't by her side and helping her grow, that he had not caused this death because he wasn't there. He says he would never have been able to love her and be her Protector forever. He had to let her go, to pass her on and let her face other things and other men. He says he had finished with her. Commitment is so fleeting sometimes, he says. There's a saint in Iasi, he says, who has failed one of her daughters. That dead bitch Parascheva, he adds, has probably failed a lot more girls than just Alina.

GADAKA asks him to charge more. He says he hates the other men who watch. Let's find out who really values these rare and special things, he says. Henry whacks up the price: $300 a minute. It's more than anyone pays for anything. Three men are left, awaiting whatever ferocious treats that may follow. He hits $500 a minute and two leave. GADAKA is left, present, incorrect. He tells Henry this is sweet. He tells him that this is as wonderful as the internet gets, as free as free speech can be. Henry tells GADAKA how Alina thought she was pregnant. GADAKA is disappointed. He could have had the baby for his own purposes, he says, it must have been his own secret child inside Alina. Henry says nothing. He stares into her webcam, wondering about this thing on the other end of the wire, wondering whose friend or neighbour or employee he is. GADAKA tells Henry he shouldn't get upset by such statements. He tells him all things become acceptable when you make your mind up that they are. Henry breathes in now. He wants to talk. He tells GADAKA that he understands what he said. He says he knows a man who has shown him it could be true, that all things can become acceptable. He says there is a Last Door in the mind which borders life's rules and restrictions. On the outside, men are truly free to find their own way, where no conscience questions their actions. Out there, he says, they can make their own rules.

GADAKA loves the phrase – The Last Door. He says he too must have passed through that Door. He asks Henry how far the man on top of Alina has passed through The Last Door, and Henry says that the man can no longer see it behind him.

GADAKA likes the answer.

He asks: 'Is Alina yours?'

'No.'

'But you liked her?'

'Yes.'

'You wanted her?'

'Yes.'

'Yet that man has abused her memory.'

'Yes.'

'The Last Door.'

'Yes.'

'It's so nice to be on the other side.'

'Yes.'

'Why don't you kill him?'

Nothing shocks Henry Sender. He considers that, at this moment, there's nothing that could scare him or make him want to hide. He tells GADAKA that he might do it, that it might be the right thing to do. He says he has always known that death must be the easy part of life.

GADAKA says he can see the handle of a revolver poking out from the top of the tattooed man's jeans. Henry looks, and sees it. PROVIDERANDDENIER forever. He pulls it out and rolls Shuff onto his back so that he lies beside Alina, one arm flopping across her abdomen. He puts the weapon into Shuff's face, cocks the hammer and looks to GADAKA. GADAKA tells him to do it. Henry pushes the gun into Shuff's mouth, forcing open his teeth. Shuff grunts, bites a little. He's dreaming of falling into darkness, a sea of black ink, his head severed and being shot again and again and again. His eyes flicker with every impact.

GADAKA tells Henry to continue. Henry pushes it in further, Shuff's sleepy, drunken drool now wetting the chamber. GADAKA commends him for his work so far. He tells him to continue, to go through The Last Door and join the club. Henry sees the Door again. He's seen it for hours. He's seen it in London, in Iasi, on a plane, in a bar, a club, on the news, hanging beside him, and he sees it, invisible, on the screen in front. The images swirl in his mind. He feels dizzy, as if racing and spinning through somewhere. Shuff feels a bullet tear into his mind, ripping through the forces which drive him, pounding out of the back of his head, releasing and diluting the immense power of his life. His eyelids ball up in pain, their host beaten by the ferocious, short, violent journey of a piece of lead. Henry thinks of tilting Shuff's head to one side. He looks at Alina, at the slight, hard twist in her snapped spine.

He pulls the gun away. He won't do it. He won't kill a man. Henry Sender won't kill anyone. He hasn't got the gene. He turns to the screen. There's a pause. GADAKA masturbates. He stops. He is lost. Henry tells him he won't shoot Shuff. GADAKA replies that he is witnessing a transition, that he believes something great is occurring in Henry. Henry says he can feel that he is going somewhere new, that he is arriving at something. He looks at the webcam, at the relentless GADAKA, the only other entity alive who sees a solidity within Henry Sender.

'Henry,' he writes. 'My dear Henry.'

Henry reaches to the screen and hikes the price. He's fearless. He wants to push GADAKA to the limit, to dry the fuel which propels him. It's now $1,000 dollars a minute. How far will GADAKA go? How far will Henry go? They are playing some kind of chicken, and Henry Sender, forever out of control, now wants to win.

GADAKA laughs. He jerks again like a man on a rope, a man who talks a world of horror with a single hand, who endorses it with the other. He asks Henry does he have anything he wants to do? He asks is there a need within him?

Henry says yes. GADAKA asks him what it is, and Henry doesn't answer. GADAKA says he will answer for him, that he will give him an awesome task that will guarantee he shoots through The Last Door. He says Henry must put the gun to his own head and kill himself.

15

GADAKA's wife has retired after a long evening of shouting about bills, of debating the shame and pain which she and her husband and children are having to face. Martha's hungrier than she can remember being, having decided to reduce the family's intake of food in the hope it will help her pay an angry, red electricity demand. She thinks how there was a time, only a couple of years ago, when she didn't know that a red bill was actually red. She thought it was a turn of phrase, something only the unemployed and irresponsible knew anything about.

Her husband had told her how his trip abroad had proved fruitless, that his Romanian contact had let him down in typical eastern fashion, and that he was working desperately yet confidently on another way of making things work. He held her tightly as she wept. She told him she had thought about taking her own life. GADAKA said she must never say that again, and that he was sure things would be all right. Everyone goes through bad patches, he said. He told her he was fearless and cunning and willing to do whatever it took to get what was needed.

Hugging her shaking body, he couldn't wait for her to go to bed. He wanted nothing more than her tired old face to be asleep, so that his dark day could really begin. He hadn't seen Alina online since he had returned home, and he was hoping that tonight would be the night when she turned up again on camera, after reflecting on what had been done to her and realising that GADAKA had taught her something valuable about life. He wanted to see what the filthy shit Romanian whore would say to him when she saw his name again. It gave him pleasure to think that he had spotted his opportunity, taken her for a fool and robbed her of her time, body and mind.

As his wife and children fell asleep, hoping their dreams would take them away from their waking misery, he dimmed the light and went looking for her. He was truly disappointed to find her dead, but only because he would never see what bad and broken English words she wanted to say to him. Still, he thought, at least he did get some kind of a reaction. Her death, he thought, was her twisted tribute to him. The little bitch, he thought, hadn't been able to cope with a man of his maturity. She was no fucking loss. She was fucking finished anyway. Fucked stupid, fucked to death. Plenty more beautiful, cheap, white, eastern Alinas out there, all ready and willing to be screwed. Christ, he thought, half of Europe is coming down with them, these smiling, easy substitutes for the teenagers who slept within his house.

Now GADAKA had spotted another opportunity, a fresh idea to thrill that part of his brain which thrived on the vile and taboo and anything that people said was too much, too far, too sick, too hard to even believe. He took the opportunity without question. Money would not stand in his way. He was way beyond all that. His trail of secret credit cards could feed this hungry, ever-grazing machine for an age, and that was all that mattered now.

He knows tonight what it was that changed in him when he became the man he is today, when he killed his conscience and resigned himself to the fact that he is a man who has nurtured a naked evil inside him, who has thrilled at the contempt of others. Henry had recognised it too. GADAKA feels how The Last Door makes so much sense to him, that the words clarify the jumbled, struggling identities of his mind. He feels tonight as if he is so far through The Last Door that he can't even see it behind him any more. It is like some kind of race for the bravest of the brave, and he knows he can win.

GADAKA I can tell you're interested.
HENRY   Yes.
GADAKA Do you feel that you have passed through The Last Door?
HENRY   Something like that.
GADAKA Why don't you go further, and keep on going? Do it in style. Take it as far as it can go. See where it leads, where it ends. I know you're interested.
HENRY   Yes.
GADAKA How many bullets are in the gun?
HENRY   Wait.
GADAKA Okay.
HENRY   Just one.
GADAKA Poetic.
HENRY   Yes.
GADAKA I will be the one to tell the tale. I'm the witness to your courage.
HENRY   Yes.
GADAKA Tell me honestly – did you love her?
HENRY   Yes.
GADAKA And what of him? Who is he to you?
HENRY   My Protector.
GADAKA Did he tell you about The Last Door?
HENRY: Yes.
GADAKA Did you enjoy what he did on the other side?

HENRY	I don't know. I saw violence. Excess. I saw everything. It was strange. Almost funny.
GADAKA	And did you enjoy it? His violence, and excess? The almost funny?
HENRY	Yes. I felt as if I was strong when I was with him, because he was there.
GADAKA	What a tribute. He has a great power. I can tell.
HENRY	Yes. He has no fear.
GADAKA	I understand.
HENRY	He has killed people. An old man and maybe a baby. Others too.
GADAKA	Obscene.
HENRY	Yes. Before I met him, I didn't know anyone could do that or think that way.
GADAKA	Oh, there are many of us – many with our funny excesses.
HENRY	Yes. I know now.
GADAKA	This, Henry, would be your tribute to him. Your own ultimate achievement and excess. What else is there after this? Your beautiful Alina is gone. Only excess can reload such a void. You can exceed all the others now, you can go beyond them.
HENRY	Yes.
GADAKA	Take everything you want now.
HENRY	I know. He believes that everything is your own. You just have to take it.
GADAKA	I understand. I like this man.
HENRY	Shuff.
GADAKA	Shuff. I like Shuff.
HENRY	Yes.
GADAKA	Henry. I want to see that you are through

	The Last Door, so far through that you cannot fall back and lose.
HENRY	Yes.
GADAKA	I want you to do this thing. Show me that The Last Door is far behind you. Show me it's so far behind that you can't even see it.
HENRY	I want you to pay $5,000 per minute. It's the outer limit. It's your commitment.
GADAKA	That is easy to me. So be it, Henry.
HENRY	Wait.
GADAKA	Of course.
HENRY	That's it.
GADAKA	Good.
HENRY	Good.
GADAKA	Now, Henry.
HENRY	Yes.
GADAKA	Now.
HENRY	Okay.
GADAKA	That's it. To your temple. Mmmmmm. That's it. So hot. Now do it, Henry. Do it for me.
HENRY	Watch.
GADAKA	Mmmmmm. I'm watching baby.
HENRY:	Goodbye.
GADAKA:	Farewell, Henry. I love you.
HENRY:	Gadaka?
GADAKA:	Yes, my love?
HENRY:	You're a wanker.

Gadaka's wife woke to the roar. She heard the computer crash against the wall, the shouts of pain from her husband's study. She heard him curse and punch the desk. She heard the thuds as he banged his head off the wall. She knew all along that he too was feeling the pain of their circumstances, but now he was really starting to show it. It comforted her. She knew he couldn't hold it in. He had to crack, to release some of the tension. It was good for him. His fury gave her relief. He would now have some relief too. She knew that he was the man she loved and that he would do only his best for her and the children. She knew he had recently taken her wedding dress out of its box and she knew it was because he wanted to remind himself of happier times, and of his love for her. She was comforted, and fell back into a deep sleep.

16

Henry drinks vodka and counts the thousands of dollars in his online account. He stands up soberly, whole, and scans the small flat. It is brighter, the sun is rising. He places the revolver tenderly on Shuff's broad, breathing chest. PROVIDERANDDENIER. He looks around and he too breathes in, steady and calm, surrounded by the madness of this voyage.

As the sun appears high above the dirty grey tower opposite, he wonders how many nights Alina had watched that daily beginning from here, in this room, while hard at work. He is not afraid to kiss her lips for the first time. They feel soft and kind. Shuff was wrong.

Henry takes Shuff's wrist, wrapping his fingers around it, blocking out one Article of Faith. PROVIDERANDDENIER. He pulls his heavy, sleeping, living hand from Alina's stillness. He moves it softly onto his chest. PROVIDERANDDENIER. He scans the flat again. He sees boxes in a wardrobe in one of the barren bedrooms, boxes of a family's story, folded away, out of sight. He finds a white sheet, Gogu's sheet, unwashed since her father had slept on it here for the final time. He gently removes the last of her clothing and lifts her, light and free. He wraps her tightly, takes her safely in his arms and leaves.

Alina is carried carefully and slowly down ten flights of stairs. He takes her out onto the street and begins to mingle with the city as it comes to life. He walks slowly, gently, towards the centre, calm and quiet. A trickle of unsure people give him the space he needs as he passes. He takes her over a bridge, across the watery barrier which had separated her from her Saint. He walks into the morning city centre, noticed less and less.

One mile away, the great doors of the Metropolitan Cathedral are open and welcoming. Inside it is warm and fair, empty and undisturbed. Henry sees the huge silver coffin, lying in state amid four gold posts, the immovable, priceless resting place of a woman who has loved all the sons and daughters of her city for a thousand years. Tears do not fall from Henry Sender as he lifts Alina to its side and lays her down. They fall from him as he descends to his knees and prays that this young girl be protected for evermore. He weeps when he learns that St Parascheva had told her tired and scared flock *I am light, and I am sun.*

Outside, he sits on a low wall and watches the people. He wonders how many of them want to stay where they are and how many want to go? How many of them have the chance to begin again, to go to a new place to try and take the hopes and dreams which are rightfully theirs? He thinks how he now knows what he will do. He will go to the place that he knows is home. He is going to find the people who have loved him, and love them back. He doesn't believe he could have come to feeling as strong as this on his own.

Henry rubs at his face as he thinks how he had admired Shuff, how he had admired that part of his sure mind which relished living, that deep well of power which beat back death. Shuff had made him laugh and look and take and learn and listen, and Henry had watched him Provide and Deny. But that admiration is all gone now, faded in the light of day. Shuff was the show, and Henry has walked away.

Something changed as Henry took power over Shuff, as he

crept up on a sleeping giant with his fate in his hands. Somehow a full feeling had unified the states of his mind, and it is still there, lurking around, threatening remedy, telling him he can take power again. He feels ready now for a battle.

When he checks out of the hotel in which he did not stay, he thanks the man at the desk. He tells him that the man he was with has not returned from a night out and he doesn't know where he is. The man says this is fine. He tells Henry not to worry, that everything is okay. Henry leaves and hails a cab. He tells the driver to take him to the train station.

On the way, they pass a newly decorated orphanage. Small children, sore, cut, pale, dying, play behind the high wire. Henry has the driver stop. He calls in and, with the swipe of a card, he gives $5,000 to the cause, turning a minute of madness into months of miracles. The beautiful old woman whom one could trust with one's life conducts the transaction. She has tears in her eyes. She tells him that he has done a wonderful thing. She says he's a saint.

Henry doesn't notice the photograph of a living, giving Matilda Sender on the wall. He wouldn't have been surprised to see it. He would have told the woman in the orphanage that Matilda was a saint, and that he had prayed for her, that he was going to see her again. Henry thanks the old woman and goes back to his taxi. He pauses. He looks up at the risen sun.

Epilogue

Shuff Sheridan had awoken in maze of confusion, a gun in his hand, a live and a dead body missing from his view. He searched for a note, for a reason why Henry would have left without him, but he found nothing, no directions. He finished his vodka, stared out at the grey tower block across the street, and left.

His memory had failed. He knew he had been on another wild night and remembered having his hands on someone's body. As he walked to the city centre, one of Gogu's small shirts stretched across his torso, he tried to recall if that body had been male or female, to recall what kind of assault it was that he had conducted.

It came to him as he sat quietly on the plane to London, after a long train journey, after hours of sitting and drinking and smoking, lonely and bored, tired and trying to handle the ever-burgeoning pain from his sledgehammered testicles. It had been Yan, that fucken Russian. Shuff had returned to the nightclub, high on stolen chemistry, and raged into that side room with an awesome, driven, nuclear power. He had found Yan sitting, bandaged, licking his wounds with two sympathetic protectors. Shuff had ripped the stolen shirt from his own body, exposing his dedication to his word, and Yan had wailed in terror. PROVIDERANDDENIER. Shuff had remembered what he had told the Russian he would do to him if he crossed him, and he had told him then that he would keep his promise.

He remembered that he had killed one of the men with one of the two bullets, and had beaten the other to a bloody end with the wild whip of that pistol. He had crashed Yan to the floor, onto his front, kicking and praying, and torn his back open with the jagged neck of a broken beer bottle. He had raised it and thumped it down, hard, over and over again as he had beaten his way through to the vertebrae.

Shuff rubbed at his temples, a hot sweat gathering as he remembered his thick fists around exposed bones, wrenching and loosening bloody chunks within his dying victim's back, and he wondered if he'd shredded, even severed, the spinal cord within. He had leaned down to Yan's ear and softly whispered: 'I fucken warned you, big lad.'

In a London airport, they had met him, an army of officials, a regiment of rules. They cornered him with guns as the endless gang – more determined than truth itself – tried to arrest Digby 'Shuff' Sheridan. They tore him to the ground as he sent them soaring, and they tore him to the ground again and again and again and again.

He sits now, silent, unvisited, caged in an unbreakable square, allowed out only to walk in pointless circles alone within a small, sealed prison yard. They call him The Killer Of Old Frank The Fess, The Monster Who Fed His Inbred Baby To A Dog, and they say he's the madman who took on a Russian Mafia boss, all by himself, and and ripped up his spine with his bare hands.

The Monster looks now through the narrow window out of which, with Romanian consent, he will look for the rest of his life. He fixes his balls, and he is thirsty, and busy with his thoughts. The Last Door is just a memory.

Also available from
Blackstaff Press

JASON JOHNSON
Woundlicker

'Belfast came up with the Titanic, the Troubles, the car bomb, kneecapping, Ulster fries and big fucken sinks. What the fuck is all that about? I mean, it's been great for churches and off-licences and journalists and all, but that's it.'

Maverick misfit Fletcher Fee is being recorded. And he's got a lot to say. Incensed by attacks on 'Wee Blondie', his teenage neighbour, and by the senseless murder of his only friend, Karim, Fee responds with increasingly violent acts of revenge that threaten to derail the uneasy peace process in Northern Ireland.

Living on the edge, Fee moves invisibly through a gritty post-ceasefire Belfast, confounding the police and paramilitaries and exposing a dark network of lies and collusion. But how far will the mysterious authorities let him go? And why?

A monologue presented in the form of a classified British government report, *Woundlicker* is a page-turning thriller from an exciting new voice in Irish fiction.

ISBN 0-85640-774-7

£6.99

www.blackstaffpress.com

Also available from
Blackstaff Press

MARK O'SULLIVAN
Enright

It is 1921, and the Irish War of Independence is
drawing to a close. In a small Tipperary town, RIC Sergeant
Tom Enright fights the rebels – and his own demons.

Mark O'Sullivan's gripping novel is as forceful as
the character of Enright himself. The story hovers between
the real and the imagined, between tenderness and violence,
between myth and memory. Enright's voice haunts, revolts,
amuses, and ultimately reveals the secret of survival –
defiant tenacity.

'a challenging and original author'
Books Ireland

'the truth and lies of life rarely meet
with such provoking starkness'
Irish Times

'impeccable mastery of narrative and dialogue'
Sunday Tribune

ISBN 0-85640-773-9
£6.99

www.blackstaffpress.com

Coming soon from
Blackstaff Press

GARBHAN DOWNEY

Running Mates

Enraged by revelations from her fiancé's stag night, Derry judge Lou Johnston launches herself into the race for the Irish presidency. But her plans receive a rude setback when her old flame Stan pitches his hat into the ring.

As more contenders emerge, Lou and Stan find themselves enmeshed in the most crooked, underhand election of all time.

An irresistibly funny new novel that lifts the lid on the fast-talking, double-dealing, and often comic world of cross-border politics.

PRAISE FOR GARBHAN DOWNEY

'The best Northern Ireland political novel of the century.'

Sunday Times

'Downey has once again constructed a world of rogues and crooks that Dickens would have been proud to have created.'

Irish News

'A gem ... this new author is eagle-eyed and as sharp as a lance'

Belfast Telegraph

ISBN 0-85640-799-2

£6.99

www.blackstaffpress.com